The Tainted Teacup

MICHELLE BUSBY

Patent Print Books
Panama City Beach, Florida

THE TAINTED TEACUP

Published by PATENT PRINT BOOKS
www.patentprintbooks.com
PATENT PRINT BOOKS and the fingerprint colophon are registered trademarks of PATENT PRINT BOOKS

First Edition: 2020
Printed in the United States of America

ISBN 978-0-578-67062-4
Library of Congress Control Number: 2020904180

10   9   8   7   6   5   4   3   2   1

Dedicated to my children,
who were the most difficult mysteries
I ever tried to solve.

In Appreciation

I want to express my appreciation for those who had a part in the inspiration and completion of this book: my publisher, my editors, my proofreaders, my fellow sleuths, my friends, and especially my family.

Introduction

"Yes, that's it!" said the Hatter with a sigh, "It's always tea time ..."

"Take some more tea," the March Hare said to Alice, very earnestly.

"I've had nothing yet," Alice replied in an offended tone, "so I can't take more."

"You mean you can't take less," said the Hatter. "It's very easy to take more than nothing."

~ Lewis Carol,
Alice in Wonderland

HAVE YOU EVER WONDERED how and why drinking tea and observing teatime have figured so prominently in history and literature?

Teatime refers to the time of day at which tea is taken—somewhere between late afternoon and early evening— to fill the gap between the noon meal and the evening meal. It is characterized by simple snacks of bread and butter, cakes, pastries, or tiny sandwiches paired with a hot beverage—tea.

Its invention is credited with Anna Maria, Duchess of Bedford, who conceived of it in the 1800s as a social event for the wealthy upper crust of England. By the 1900s, it was observed by both upper- and middle-class citizens. Somewhere along the way, teatime lost its formality and was brought to the masses in the form of tearooms, which were similar to coffeehouses, and at which people of all walks of life could gather and "decompress" from the day's stresses to dunk a pastry and sip a cup of the tasty infusion.

Tea originated during the 3rd century AD in Southwest China, where it was a medicinal drink. Legend tells of a great Emperor of China who decreed that his subjects boil their water to prevent disease. One day, some leaves floated into his cup, and he didn't remove them. He found the taste of the water infused with the brewed leaves delicious and stimulating.

Tea drinking spread quickly throughout the East Asian countries. It was introduced in Europe during the 16th century by Portuguese priests, and its popularity exploded from there to the entire world. Now, tea is the most consumed beverage in the world, second only to water. In addition to drinking, teas (especially herbal tea mixtures) can be used in medicinal remedies, salves, or wound compresses. (I saved my dog from succumbing to parvo by dosing him regularly over several days with an herbal tea blend until he could be seen by a veterinarian.) For those with a mystical bent, the dregs in the bottom of a teacup can be read by a "seer" in a process called tassiomancy to divine one's fortune.

There are many types of teas: black, white, green, and herbal among them, but most are made mainly from the bitter leaves of plants. Harvested tea leaves are processed by grinding, pounding, pan-frying, oxidizing, fermenting, brewing, boiling, steeping, and any number of novel ways in which to extract the taste or enhance the restorative properties. Herbal teas are not exclusively made from the leaves; they are frequently brewed from flowers, stems, bark, and the fruits of plants, and often they are combined and used as medicines, as well as tasty sipping beverage.

Tea's popularity spans all cultures. The Irish drink it throughout the day; they are the second biggest tea consumers in the entire world. In Asian cultures, the brewing and serving of tea is a tradition, and tea ceremonies are highly ritualized and revered as a symbol of peace and beauty. At one time in America, tea was a commodity as valuable as currency and was as coveted as bootleg liquor during prohibition. (Remember the Boston Tea Party in 1773?)

In West Africa, the "gunpowder" tea drinking ritual is a rite of passage for determining the mettle of a man (or woman). They brew it strong and bitter and serve it piping hot in a shot glass. The visitor must endure the highly caffeinated substance without complaint through three rounds. The first drink is unsweetened and symbolizes the trials and harshness of life. The second brewing of the same leaves is milder and sweetened with a touch of sugar. It symbolizes a more pleasant life of patient endurance. The third and final preparation is poured into a shot glass packed with sugar. The person who is determined and can endure to the last shot is deemed trustworthy enough to be called a friend. I participated in this ritual during a short trip to a village outside Senegal. I was called a friend … but I didn't sleep for three days afterward!

Finally, there is the age-old debate between coffee and tea. Both have their pros and cons, but the bottom line is that most people prefer one or the other. For those who choose to abstain from drinking either, Thomasina Watson recommends you try an herbal blend with fresh, clean water. What's my take? I listen to Tommie Watson.

~ *Michelle Busby*

Chapter One

"That's it," said the Hatter with a sigh: "it's always tea-time."
~ Lewis Carol,
Alice in Wonderland

WHAT CAN HAPPEN IN 13 MINUTES?

At 12:15 on an unseasonably warm February Monday in North Florida, Ms. Coral Beadwell entered Watson's Reme-Teas and ordered a cup of the special house blend.

At 12:28, Coral lay dead on the floor with her head in the puddle of caramel-colored liquid that had spilled from her favorite teal and yellow teacup, her fingers still clutching the broken ceramic handle.

What can happen in 13 minutes? Murder.

Chapter Two

THOMASINA "TOMMIE" WATSON slammed the dark grey stone grinder into the matching granite bowl with a fierceness the delicate herbs did not deserve. The rectangular ottoman she was using as a counter responded with a slight bounce as she pounded the pestle into the mortar over and over. Unable to sleep, she had laid a wooden cutting board on the footstool so she could sit on the loveseat as she prepared the herbs for a soothing bedtime tea.

Her eyes misted yet again, recalling the events that had unfolded on Monday, February 11, 2019—just 12 hours before—when Coral Beadwell had died on the floor of Tommie's shop. She sighed raggedly. *Has it really only been twelve hours?* she wondered, absently wiping the tears away with the sleeve of her night shirt.

Monday had started out business as usual at Watson's Reme-Teas, her herbal teas and natural remedies shop on Bottlebrush Boulevard in downtown Floribunda. She had happily leased it from her cousin Sanderson Harper in late October. When he was using the space, he called it Sandy's Sandwiches and sold simple cold cuts on bread with a bag of chips and a canned soda. It was not a booming business, but it was something he could do when he had down time from being the Floral County Coroner.

The shop, under Tommie's creative rebranding and renovation efforts, had begun to show a decent profit. It seemed the Floribunda townsfolk liked having a resident herbalist who could make natural remedies and cosmetics, as well as delicious, healthy tea blends.

Less than two weeks ago, however, on the 30th of January, Beverly Cantrell from Floral Real Estate had dropped a bomb on her with a single phone call.

"Tommie, darling. It's Beverly," she had purred.

"Hello, Beverly. What can I do for you?" Tommie had asked while she measured out chamomile flowers and willow bark for soaking to extract the calming and analgesic agents. The macerated herbs would be combined with coconut oil for a soothing acne fighting face cream, and the strained liquid would be the base for a headache remedy.

"I hate to be the bearer of potentially bad news, but your duplex has been sold." There was a lilt in her voice that had made Tommie feel Beverly enjoyed delivering bad news.

"What do you mean it's been sold?" Tommie stoppered the herb containers and sat upright on her high barstool at the prep counter in her shop.

"Well, you know our rentals are always for sale if someone should come by and want to buy them. It's in the lease agreement you signed. You remember?"

"Vaguely. I wasn't in a very good frame of mind at that time." Tommie raised her left foot and propped it on the shorter stool beside her. Her leg was still clad to the knee in the heavy black walking boot to support her broken ankle.

"Well, be that as it may, you signed it, and the duplex has been bought by a man from Dublin."

"Dublin … as in Ireland? What are you saying Beverly? What does that mean?" Tommie could feel the morning's breakfast rising into her throat. She swallowed reflexively to quell the nausea.

"I really couldn't say at this point, but yes, Ireland. Imagine that! He bought it sight-unseen over the internet and wired us the money today. My understanding is that he is moving from Dublin and will be taking up residence here at the end of next week. The good news is we have a *few* other rentals available now, but they won't last long, so don't be caught short. You'll be given a full three weeks to move out, so you can start your new lease on the first of March.

"Your initial deposit may be returned, or you may apply it toward the new rental. Your pet deposit was non-refundable, of course, and you *will* have to make new applications for both of your dogs and pay a new deposit when you have decided on another rental. You are still responsible for the final maintenance and cleanup, to be done to the satisfaction of the new owner. You'll have to work that out with him."

Tommie could not miss the overt satisfaction and condescension in Beverly Cantrell's voice as she went through her spiel. She was a hungry shark who trolled tirelessly for her exorbitant commissions and excessive leasing agent fees.

"Beverly, how am I supposed to do all that while I'm still recovering from this broken ankle?" Tommie asked, trying to ignore the insistent throbbing in her toes from leaving the foot down too long.

"Oh, I thought surely it was healed by now. It's been over four months."

"I have nerve damage, and it's taking a lot longer to heal."

"Oh my, that's too bad. Now, don't you have an adult son nearby and some friends who can help you? They moved you in, didn't they? Well, I've got to run. Just wanted to give you a heads up. Have a nice day," she said and abruptly disconnected.

Tommie fisted her hands into her short salt and pepper hair and rested her elbows on the counter, blinking back angry tears. *Dangit all, Beverly Cantrell,* she thought, *and you, too, you mystery man from Ireland.*

Why can't you just stay in your own country?

In that one short phone call, the world, which had just returned to some semblance of normalcy, had suddenly spun out of control. Tommie knew she didn't have the money to put down on a new place to live, nor could she do the physical packing, moving, and final maintenance on the current place.

Tommie had just gotten to the point where she could comfortably hobble around without additional assistance from a wheelchair or a walker, but she was far from healed. Even with surgically placed pins and a plate, the bones of a 64-year-old didn't knit as well as they would have, were she younger. There was also the complication of the damaged nerves. Adding insult to injury, her doctor had pointed out the weight factor. After an entire life of being slim and trim during the childbearing years from her three failed marriages, Tommie's 5'2" body had inexplicably reverted to the genes of the heavy side of her family. At 200 pounds, regardless of the countless diets with which she tortured herself, the stress to her ankle was significant.

When Tommie regained control of her temper, she had done the one thing she could think of: she called her friend Maggie Kohl in Rivertown. After explaining the situation, she prayed Maggie would give her some sage advice. Maggie had.

"Tommie, let's put this in perspective like we always do when you have a crisis," she said.

Maggie meant nothing untoward in the comment, and Tommie took it as it was intended. She did, indeed, have multiple crises—as did Maggie—but together, they always figured out the solutions to their personal problems.

"I know, I know. What's this, number 24,399?" Tommie had asked with a laugh.

"No, I think it's 24,400. But who's counting?"

"OK. What can I do, Maggs? I'm financially tapped out, and I'm physically and emotionally the same," Tommie lamented.

"Just wait. We'll figure it out. Point A to point B before we try to jump to point Q."

"Right. Point A is where I'm at—January 30, 2019 in Floribunda, Florida. I'm sublimely happy in my little duplex with my dogs, loving my herbal shop, finally getting some pretty good repeat customers, but I'm not making enough to do all the deposits and stuff."

"And point B is where you need to be. But at this time, we don't *know* where you need to be, or even *when*."

"I'll have three weeks to get out of the duplex and do the final maintenance and cleanup on it once he moves in." Tommie sighed heavily, fighting to control the tears.

"Not necessarily. What'd that woman say? She couldn't really tell you what would happen, right? Maybe he won't want you to move? Maybe you can continue to rent and pay him instead?"

"I suppose."

"What's today? Wednesday? He's coming at the end of next week. That's, um … let me see … nine days away if he comes on Friday. You can chill for nine days. No need to make any plans before then. After he moves in, you must take him a goodie-filled welcome basket with a special herbal tea … the Irish do love their tea. Oh, and that sweetener you make with the honeysuckle blossoms and raw clover honey. He'll be so appreciative. You're charming, and wonderful. How can he not want you to keep living there?"

"You give me too much credit, Maggs. I'm wonderful but not that charming." Tommie chuckled despite herself.

"Oh yes, you are! Stop putting yourself down. *Fwap-fwap!*" She made slapping sounds, which caused Tommie to laugh aloud. "You're an amazing person, and Craig and I just love you so much."

"You do, you do. All right. My face is officially stinging from your smacking. I'll make up a special blend for him. Maybe even bake a banana bread or something."

"There you go. And I shall light a pink candle and pray for your success," she said in the cheerfully dramatic and musical quality her voice took on when being emphatic.

"Thank you, Maggs. I'm sure that'll do it."

"It will. Point A to point B, and he shall be your new landlord. He is point B. Believe it, and the universe shall make it so. Get to work, Tommie Watson, and concoct your magic potion for him," Maggie had commanded, making kissing noises before hanging up.

Talking with Maggie had always left Tommie in a good mood, as much for the advice as for the complete focus Maggie gave to helping solve her problems. If ever there was a true friend in the world, that friend was Maggie Kohl. Not to say that Terry Jackson and Annie Lang weren't also her true-blue friends. They absolutely were, but in different ways. Maggie had been her soul sister for more than 30 years, and they could nearly read each other's minds.

Tommie got busy and mixed up more of the sweetener she called *Honey-Honey,* which she would take the Irishman in nine days or so. Afterward, she portioned out the herbs to make his tea blend: lavender and chamomile flowers for a mood elevator and to reduce stress and muscle tension, lemon balm leaf for calmness, basil leaf to combat irritability and fatigue, and a pinch of powdered cardamom as an aphrodisiac to make Tommie seem more alluring to him. She crushed the seeds, bruised the flowerheads and leaves to release their oils, put the mixed herbs into a zipper lock plastic bag, and labeled it *Laid-back Landlord.*

She did a Google search and found that the Irish prefer milk with their tea instead of lemon. Tommie planned to make him a special creamer that would ensure he had a good night's rest with pleasant dreams while he thought about her living situation. She set aside whole nutmeg and a small vial of rose water. Just before she took him the welcome basket, she would grind out ½ teaspoon of the nutmeg, combine it with one tablespoon of the rose water, and mix it into eight ounces of fresh milk. She called it *Dreamer Creamer.*

Once her preparations were done, Tommie had brewed a cup of her homemade *Blues Reme-Tea,* made with an infusion of St. John's wort, spearmint leaves, nettle leaves, lemon balm, dried oregano, and basil leaves steeped in filtered water, and sweetened with 100% grade A dark maple syrup.

Nine days. Tommie had felt prepared after Maggie's pep talk, and she believed she could endure the next nine days. She sipped the warm tea and savored the sweetness of the maple syrup. She found herself feeling much better. Sadly, her respite had been short-lived.

Chapter Three

THE NEW OWNER ARRIVED on Wednesday afternoon
instead of Friday, while Tommie was still at her shop. He
took an Uber to Floral Real Estate, retrieved his keys,
exchanged pleasantries with Beverly Cantrell and the
owner, Charles Williams, and then he asked for directions
to his new home on Camelia Street. Beverly immediately
insisted on driving him—and his emotional support
dog—to the duplex. As they pulled into the left unit
carport, he thanked her for the lift but neglected to invite
her in. She backed her car out onto the road in a huff and
sped away.

That she was nonplussed did not bother Mr.
Finbar Holmes in the least. Being European and 71 years
old, he was often abrupt with others. Besides that, he
possessed keen instincts about people, and his take on
Miss Beverly Cantrell was entirely accurate. He had no
interest in befriending her or her pretentious associate.

The first thing Holmes had done when she drove

off was put the dog on the grass and let him do his business. A well-behaved Jack Russell Terrier, Sherlock (yes, his name was Sherlock) stayed right by his master's side while Finbar inspected the grounds all the way around the duplex. Not quite finding them to his satisfaction, he made a few notes in a small journal he carried: 1. Hire lawn service. 2. Have a privacy fence erected around entire back garden. 3. Install a pet portal for Sherlock. 4. String up a clothesline.

With Sherlock's immediate necessaries taken care of, Holmes unlocked the unit's rear door and entered the dwelling. His trusty little dog examined the rooms along with him, sniffing the corners, hoping for any sign of vermin, for he loved chasing mice. Finding none, he gave an audible doggie sigh and settled himself on the painted concrete floor.

That will need covering, Finbar noted. *Sherlock much prefers wood flooring, as do I. These walls cry for warmth, as well.* He jotted in his journal: 5. Decoration supplies—wood for flooring and paneling, wood stain, Tung oil, brushes, paint, sandpaper, rags. 6. Tools—circular saw, hammer, nails, power drill, screws. 7. Necessities—towel, bathing cloths, toiletries, bedding, air mattress, cooking essentials, food and drink.

Putting the journal on the kitchen counter, Holmes went back out to the garden, leaving the door open for Sherlock. He dragged the faded blue resin Adirondack chair that he had found on the covered patio into the grass and sat down, basking in the sun. He pulled out his cell phone, made a number of calls, and placed several online orders.

By the time Tommie left her shop at 6:30 p.m., Finbar Holmes had already arranged for all the items on his short list to be completed. A white and orange Home Depot truck had come and gone by 2:00. Two burly workers had stacked everything on the back patio. Finbar paid them generous tips and brought the power tools inside, leaving the bundled wood planks under the cover of the patio. A car had arrived at 2:30 with two women who delivered eight blue canvas Walmart totes full of groceries, cookware, and other household sundries. Finbar had tipped them as well.

When Tommie got home that night, it was already dark, and she was lost in thought. She did not notice the lumber on the patio or the chair in the grass, nor did she have reason to turn on the patio light and look outside because her dogs Zed and Red did their business on training pads placed on large rubber mats.

She greeted her pets, changed out their dirty pads, and fed them their dinner—dry dog food topped with some shredded chicken breast and rice she had prepared in the slow cooker. She served herself a chicken breast with rice and nibbled on her meal as she experimented with a new banana nut bread recipe for the man's arrival on Friday of the following week. With the television broadcasting *Wheel of Fortune* in the background, she didn't hear any noises from the unit on the other side of the wall.

Finbar Holmes and his canine companion heard no noises either. They were both fast asleep on a deluxe air mattress in the back bedroom, exhausted from jet lag after the long plane trip and the six-hour time difference between Ireland and Florida.

On Thursday morning, Tommie awoke at 10:00, thanks to the *Blues Reme-Tea* she had drunk the night before. She hurriedly showered, dressed, and applied a little bit of makeup. Warming a few slices from the loaf of banana nut bread and slathering them with butter, she packed them in a plastic container along with some soda crackers and cheddar cheese and headed to her car to drive to Watson's.

Just before noon, her friend Sarah Beth Brewster entered Tommie's shop through the adjoining side door. Sarah Beth ran Brewster's Coffee Shoppe. Since her main business hours were 6:00 a.m. to 12:00 p.m., and Watson's were 12:00 p.m. to 6:00 p.m., she and Tommie were like shift workers. They both rented their shops from Beverly Cantrell and Charles Williams at Floral Real Estate, and they each disliked them immensely. Charles, in particular, had an annoying habit of coming in several times a week to inspect the units, and he never failed to complain about some contrived infraction.

"Mrs. Brewster, your coffee makers are set too high. I burned my mouth this morning," he said one day.

"Then learn to blow your mug to cool it down," Sarah Beth had replied.

"Ms. Watson, I believe I saw a roach in one of your jars of house blend tea," he reported one afternoon.

"Oh, yes. I put roaches in for added protein to promote vim and vigor," Tommie had quipped.

Charles Williams had just left Brewster's before Sarah Beth came through the door. The women had duplicate keys made at Home Depot so they could keep an eye on each other's shops.

"Word of warning," Sarah Beth cautioned. "His majesty is on the loose."

"Crap. What'd he say today, Sarah Beth?"

"He said the coffee was bitter, and his stomach was upset."

"And what'd *you* say, Sarah Beth?"

"I politely told him to go to the restroom and blow it out his ..."

"You did not!" Tommie exclaimed.

"No ... but I wanted to. I said he could always go to *Watson's* and get some of your *Tender Tummy Tea* to calm it down."

"No! Did you really? That wasn't very nice, trying to send him to me."

Sarah Beth snickered at her reaction. "I didn't, Tommie. Just teasing. I actually hope his stomach *is* upset. Maybe he'll leave you alone today. How're things going, by the way?"

"It's Thursday. I wonder if that Irish guy will come in tomorrow," Tommie had remarked.

"Are you ready for him?"

"Yes … and no. I test-baked a new banana nut bread and made a special tea to take him. If he's just getting in on Friday afternoon or Saturday, though, I think I'll wait until Monday evening. Give him a chance to get over jet lag and be in a better mood."

Sarah Beth pinched off a corner of Tommie's bread and popped it in her mouth. "Great idea. Oh, yum. Tasty stuff! After you give him his goodies, what'll you do then?"

"Then I'll beg him to let me stay, and if he says I can't, then I guess I'll have to find another place to live, and I'll have to give up the shop to Charles," she moaned.

"Oh, no, you will *not!*" Sarah Beth slammed her hand down on the counter. "If it comes to that, I will loan you the money to get in another house. You must *not* let Charles get his hands on your shop. He'll put me out of business, too."

Tommie was surprised at the depth of emotion Sarah Beth had displayed. She was normally pleasant and easygoing. A svelte, attractive woman with naturally curly shoulder-length light auburn hair and dark jade green eyes, she exuded an unselfconscious confidence and grace. At 5'4" and 55 years old, she was in incredible physical condition, due to her morning workouts at the gym.

Her husband Gary worked for the Floribunda

School Board, and they were financially secure. As a couple, they had one downside: their only child was a morose young man of 25 with depression who still lived with them. He didn't seem at all like he belonged to beautiful Sarah Beth. *I guess everyone has some kind of albatross,* Tommie thought and was instantly ashamed of herself in light of Sarah Beth's offer to help her find another place to live.

"Thank you, Sarah Beth. That means a lot to me." Tommie had been genuinely touched.

"Gotta stick together, right?" Hearing the jingle of the little bell over the door which signaled a customer, Sarah Beth gave Tommie a quick hug and disappeared into her own shop to close up.

Tommie always opened in time for the daily lunch crowd to stop in. She served no food, but patrons brown-bagged it at the little round tables while enjoying the hot or iced teas she prepared. When her customers went back to their jobs and the shop was quiet, Tommie spent her time making special order herbal remedies, as well as a variety of tonics, salves, and beauty products which she advertised for sale on a set of low bookcases near the display window.

Thursday was no different, and she forgot her woes in the faces of the smiling clientele who chatted with her and praised her latest house blends. February being Valentine's Day month, her newest were *Fruity Friendship*—with bits of dried apricots, cherries, and peaches in a sweet Honeybush tea—and *Romantic Red*—a customer favorite of Red Rooibos and red rose buds, with mint leaves hand-tied around jasmine flowers and served in white teacups to show off the blossoming petals that unfurled as they steeped in the boiling water.

Five hours later and bone weary, Tommie had returned to her home, fed the dogs and herself, and retired to the bedroom to watch a movie on television. Again, there was no noise from the unit next door. She had no idea Finbar Holmes had already taken up residence.

Friday had passed much the same way. Tommie left for the shop around 10:00, and Finbar considerately began his renovations as soon as her dogs announced their owner had left. He, himself, wondered how he would handle the issue of her occupation of the adjacent unit. He decided to continue decorating his unit while she was gone and wait for her to make contact. Then, he would come to a conclusion, based on his first face-to-face impression of her. Thus far, he found no objections with the level of noise from either her or her dogs. *Time will tell,* he decided as he nailed another paneling strip to the wall. *Time will tell.*

On Saturdays, Watson's and Brewster's usually kept the same hours at both shops: 9:00 a.m. to 4:00 p.m. They both sold beverages but were not in competition.

"Coffee drinkers are not tea drinkers, and vice versa," Sarah Beth had remarked when she first met the new shop owner back in October of 2018.

"That's a good point," Tommie had agreed, pulling her wheelchair around with her good leg while she removed the awful vinyl covers from the tables and cleaned all the exposed hard surfaces with an alcohol and hydrogen peroxide mixture.

Thereafter, theirs had blossomed into a congenial and cooperative relationship. Tommie was extremely relieved. There were few available retail spaces for rent in Floribunda—just like the housing—and she was lucky that her cousin decided to quit selling his horrible sandwiches. But, when she learned the business next door was a coffee shop, she had worried there would be problems between them. Instead, she had found an ally in Sarah Beth, with Charles Williams their common enemy. He was equally rude and nasty to both of them.

"What's his deal anyway?" Tommie had asked.

"He wants these two side-by-side properties," Sarah Beth responded.

"Why?"

"He's greedy. You know they're prime pieces of real estate now since the hurricane came through and destroyed so much of our downtown area. Somebody offered Charles more rent for them as one store. He'd like to buy them and combine them to make more money."

"He can't do that. My cousin Sanderson owns both of these spaces, and unless he's changed his mind, he doesn't want to sell them. He can't. They're Harper family property."

"Really? I didn't know that. Interesting. But, don't you pay rent for the shop?"

"Yes, I do … to Floral Real Estate. Sanderson lets them manage the lease."

"But, if your cousin is the owner, why do you have to pay any rent?"

"Because Sanderson Harper's a good ole boy, and he attends the First Presbyterian Church with Charles Williams. He won't sell it, but he doesn't mind making his blood relative pay for its use."

"Men. Can't live with them; can't tie 'em to a truck and drive it into the river," Sarah Beth mugged. "Speaking of men, I might have a guy who can help you get your space fixed up and organized—my son Barry. He's not so much in the personality department, but he is my child and I know he can follow directions."

"Thanks," Tommie replied, grateful for the help.

Barry had proved to be exactly as his mother had described: a medicated man-boy with little personality. He did seem to take direction well, however, and with his help, Tommie was able to get her renovations done in early November and have a successful grand opening well before Thanksgiving. In the past two months since the opening, she had progressed from wheelchair to crutches to walker to walking boot, and the herbal remedies business seemed to be thriving.

On Saturday the 9th, two days before Coral Beadwell collapsed, Tommie's thoughts had returned to the Irishman's arrival as she hobbled and limped around her shop in between customers, wiping down tables, dusting herb jars, and reordering the reference books and retail merchandise on the display shelves. *Saturday, and I still haven't seen or heard anything about the new owner. Maybe he'll come in on Sunday,* she speculated. If so, she would not know. Sunday was her day to visit her own son Kevin in Sugar Sand Beach where he lived and managed a beachside restaurant. Kevin Watson always treated his mother to lunch and a movie, and then dinner at his restaurant. She usually got home well after dark.

As far as Tommie was aware, the Irishman would order her out immediately, and she'd have just under three weeks to get resettled. She knew Kevin would come over to move her on his one day off, and her friends would help out, but Terry was a 70-year-old widow, Annie was a 60-year-old divorcee, and Craig was 66 with a bad back. Maggie was the youngest at 58, and Tommie was still somewhat crippled. Other than her 33-year-old son, they were all senior citizens. It would be a struggle; she hoped they would survive it.

She wondered if Sarah Beth had been serious about offering to front her the move-in money. Probably not without asking her husband Gary. And knowing Sanderson like she did, if he couldn't collect rent money from her, he would let somebody else have the lease.

No, if the Irishman evicted her, Tommie would certainly lose her shop, and it was the solitary source of income necessary to supplement her pitiful social security checks and the meager retirement she received from nearly 20 years as a public schoolteacher. Without the extra money, she could never rent both the shop and the duplex on Camelia Street she had called home for the past four months since the hurricane.

Back in early October of 2018, Hurricane Adam had gathered strength and hit the Florida panhandle as a monstrous category five storm. It hopped over its projected target of Sugar Sand Beach (thankfully, her son Kevin had evacuated) and landed squarely on inland Bay City. The storm wreaked havoc on the suburbs before it continued a destructive course through other outlying areas, effectively destroying the way of life as it had been known in the sleepy towns of Loblolly, Rivertown, Beavercreek, Deer Run, and Floribunda.

Tommie was living in Beavercreek when it made landfall. Her rustic tiny home was a 12-foot by 32-foot cottage she had lovingly crafted from a preconstructed side-lofted barn-style shed set up on five wooded acres near the banks of Beaver Creek. She did all the interior work herself, except for the electrical wiring, and constructed built-in furnishings to save space. An adjacent 12-foot by 20-foot shed housed her dried herbs and equipment for making teas, tinctures, decoctions, tissanes, and infusions. Together, the two shed structures formed a right angle, with a fenced grassy area for the dogs completing a 32-foor by 32-foot square.

The cottage was accessible by a two-mile dirt road which branched off a paved side street from the main highway and wound its way toward the creek. The setting was idyllic, with towering pines and majestic oaks, as well as native elderberry trees, wild blueberry bushes, creeping honeysuckle vines, and a plethora of both wild plants and cultivated herbs along the banks of the shallow creek that offered cool, clear unpolluted water.

On that morning, when it was evident the storm had changed its course, Tommie and her two elderly dogs Zed and Red had taken refuge in the Beavercreek Church of God, a brick and block building a mile up on the paved cross street. For three hours, she and about thirty of her neighbors huddled among the wooden pews with their pets and listened as the winds howled and the rains pelted the roof of the church. Then came repeated cracking sounds like gunfire and thundering, followed by ground shaking thuds.

During the brief quiet that signaled the eye passing over, some brave souls peeked through the doors, only to return with wide staring expressions and open mouths. Then, the backside of the eyewall brought the remainder of the storm. Three hours later—after the roof over the choir loft shuddered and then completely disappeared—there was an eerie silence. Hurricane Adam had finally moved on.

Tommie had ventured outside, holding tightly to the leashes of her dogs, and surveyed the damage. There were no oak trees left standing, and every single pine tree had been snapped in half. The road was impassible by vehicles, so she left her car at the church and walked the three miles home, picking her way through the downed trees and rubble. Though the cottage was still standing, a large pine tree lay across the roof. The adjoining herb workshop, with her bulk supplies, concoctions, and all her tools, was nowhere to be found.

Thankfully, it turned out the cottage had been relatively unharmed from the tree. The metal roof sustained a huge dent in the center, but there were no holes which leaked rain. The floor was wet in one area because the four-foot back barn door had nearly ripped from its hinges. Tommie repaired it by screwing it completely shut.

Because the connecting fence had been mangled beyond repair, Zed and Red could not go outside without being on their leashes. Tommie didn't mind walking them each day; it gave her something to do while she strategized getting a new workshop and replenishing her bulk herbs. Sadly, her carefully tended produce and herb garden were gone, along with all the shade trees and flowering trees, shrubs, vines, and bushes.

The electricity was off and had remained so for a month, so there was no way to pump water. Fortunately, she had stored up a large water reserve in gallon jugs up in the loft, and she had plenty of food for herself and the dogs—enough to last three to four weeks—and she knew how to cook over a campfire. She didn't relish it, but she could live without air conditioning, heat, television, and even cell phone reception … for a while.

Within days, the roads had been cleared by neighbors bearing chain saws, and generators were used to power the larger homes all around her. Tommie Watson was nothing, if not resilient. She could make it work, even without a generator. She had been on her own for six years, and she was strong and confident she could continue to live in what was left of her woods by the creek. Then, one morning when she got up to walk the dogs, she stepped outside the cottage, stumbled on some debris, and shattered her ankle.

That was the end of Tommie's independence.

A neighbor heard her screams and was able to get her to the hospital in Ag City, Alabama. Kevin and her Rivertown friends moved her to Floribunda a week later.

On that Monday night in February 2019, after Coral's death, Tommie felt like she was facing another loss of independence, and all she could do was wait for her eventual encounter with the Irish owner of her duplex.

Chapter Four

EARLY MONDAY MORNING, Tommie had yet to meet the Irishman who bought her duplex, if indeed he had even arrived, so she dressed and went to her tea shop early. Even though she was distracted and agitated, she had forced herself to stay busy. First, she tidied up the self-service tea counter which held a cream dispenser, lemons, sweeteners, disposable spoons, napkins, and loose tea strainers. Then, she emptied the trash cans, made sure the restroom was clean, and checked the retail items on the bookcases. She completed an inventory of her bulk herbs and potion making supplies in the storage room and had checked the large cooler for any outdated concoctions. After replenishing the bottled waters and cold teas in the small coolers beside the cash register, she crawled into the left front window display and had begun to shift a few of the items there.

While she was on her hands and knees in the

display, she gazed out the window at the Confederate Memorial Park and Gazebo which were directly opposite her shop on the other side of Bottlebrush Boulevard, Floribunda's Main Street. The park was a popular picnic spot, with its lush grassy area and large octagonal gazebo beneath a spreading oak tree—one of the few left standing after the hurricane. When the weather was pleasant, people frequently bought cold teas or bottled waters from her store and took them into the gazebo during their lunch hour rather than sit inside and eat.

Directly behind the gazebo was Silver Linings—a four-story, red brick, senior living facility that was formerly a fancy hotel in the 1940s. An access road—Lantana Lane—ran diagonally between the park and the facility, connecting Nandina Street and Oleander Street.

Tommie smiled. All the streets were named after flowering trees and bushes, and she thought that was charming. Floribunda was a rural community, in size somewhere between a town and a city—small enough for one to have a wide circle of friends and acquaintances, yet large enough for a Walmart. Its bucolic nature was what appealed to Tommie; she loved countryside living.

She continued gazing out the window while she repositioned the March Hare in her *Alice in Wonderland* themed display. There was parking on Lantana Lane in front of the two office buildings beside the senior facility. The UPS Store was located in the building nearest Oleander Street, and Floral Real Estate was situated right next to Silver Linings.

From their front door, both Charles Williams and Beverly Cantrell could see everyone who came in and out of Brewster's Coffee Shoppe and Watson's Reme-Teas, as well as all the other shops that lined Bottlebrush Boulevard for which they, no doubt, held the leases. Tommie could almost feel Charles watching her from his office, and her pleasant smile drooped. She shifted her gaze to the adjacent building.

From her vantage point at the UPS Store, Ms. Coral Beadwell—a 58-year old widow from one of the original founding families of Floribunda (she took her notable maiden name back after her husband died)—held an identical view of the comings and goings along the Boulevard and at the park. She could frequently be seen standing in the doorway, her head swiveling side to side as she kept tabs on who was where, doing what, and when. She was more than a trifle nosy.

Tommie liked Coral Beadwell, even though she was known to be an overbearing bully. Her behind-the-back nickname was "hard core Coral." Tommie had heard the rumors concerning the woman: she was condescending to customers she didn't care for (especially Charles Williams); she made people wait in line for an inordinate amount of time while she intentionally dragged out helping them one by one, often causing them to run late for their jobs and appointments; and she was even suspected of blatantly snooping through people's mail. The only redeeming quality she had heard was that Coral supported Kitty Kare, the local feline rescue center.

Nonetheless, she was always friendly to Tommie when she brought her sack lunch to Watson's each day. Coral had even convinced the Ladies' Charity Organization from Trinity Episcopal Church to hold their monthly meetings at Watson's Reme-Teas. The LCO drank tea and shared the sweet treats they brought with Tommie. She was happy to serve them; they filled all 28 seats in her shop and helped her business considerably by becoming frequent patrons.

Coral was definitely a creature of habit and insisted on drinking Tommie's latest house blend tea from what she claimed was her "special teacup"—a jumbo-sized teal and pale yellow ceramic container with a picture of an orange cat on one side. Tommie kept it handy on the counter by the tea caddies.

Despite Tommie's acceptance of her quirks, it was no secret Coral was at the center of fierce animosity between the employees of the two office buildings on Lantana Lane. Tommie had seen evidence of it herself. One day, she had watched as Charles stormed out of the UPS Store with Coral on his heels, flapping her arms and shaking her head. He hurried into the real estate office, clinging to a clearly damaged parcel, his shoulders hunched up almost to his ears.

Adding to the office drama, Tommie discovered there were a couple of unrequited romances constituting a tragic love triangle—perfect fodder for enquiring minds in a small town. Perched on her barstool behind the counter at Watson's, Tommie heard all about it through the lunchtime "tea-vine" (as opposed to the grapevine).

Beverly Cantrell, the money hungry real estate maven who insisted on calling herself "Miss" despite being 56 and twice-divorced, frequently visited the UPS Store. Tommie had often watched her traipsing over there in her impossibly high heels, her brightly polished fingernails gripping legal envelopes and parcels.

"Why doesn't she take her mail to the Post Office?" Tommie had asked Sarah Beth. "It's just one street over and a whole lot cheaper."

"She prefers the customer service at the UPS Store," Sarah Beth responded with a sneer.

Upon further inquiry, Tommie had learned Beverly Cantrell had a thing for Henry Erving who worked at the UPS Store with Coral Beadwell. Henry was carrying a torch for Coral, but Coral entertained no such feelings for Henry.

Resting on her elbows in the display window, Tommie shook her head as she thought about the convoluted situation.

"That's why I'm not interested in any more marriages … or even dating, for that matter. Three strikes, and I'm officially out, O Mouse," Tommie said to the stuffed dormouse sitting in the teacup on the brightly decorated table.

As she continued crawling around in "the Mad Tea-Party," Tommie heard angry voices next door at Brewster's. She checked her watch and noted it was well past time for coffee drinkers. *Sarah Beth must have a late customer,* she decided as she flipped over on her backside and carefully scooted toward the opening.

Tommie heard Brewster's door slam. Thinking she heard her own back door open, she had craned her neck up to try and peek over the bookcases. She glanced back toward the restroom. Seeing nothing, she gingerly moved forward and set her feet down on the floor, hopped over to her front door, and turned the sign from CLOSED to OPEN.

Gazing across the street, she became aware of four people: Charles Williams—crouched down beside a parked car on Lantana Lane; Beverly Cantrell—rushing through the doorway of Floral Real Estate carrying a paper sack; Coral Beadwell—walking toward Charles; and Henry Erving— sitting alone in the gazebo, peeking around the corner post.

"We're all mad here," she told the Cheshire Cat with an enigmatic grin.

As she turned around, from the corner of her eye she glimpsed a short woman exiting through the back door. The woman's hairstyle was distinctive: a dark brown pageboy with blond highlights. It was the signature hairdo of Coral's sister-in-law, Linda Beadwell.

Chapter Five

THE BELL JANGLED over the door at 12:05 that afternoon, and Beverly Cantrell wobbled in, precariously balanced on new designer heels. Grabbing a cold tea and a bottled water from the cooler, she reached toward the cash register to drop three dollars onto the counter, bumped her hand clumsily against the teacup caddies, and then disappeared out the door without a word.

At 12:15, Coral Beadwell had entered with Charles Williams. The two of them walked to the counter together. *Well, this is an interesting new corner in the love triangle*, Tommie thought, automatically reaching for Coral's favorite teacup.

"Good afternoon, Ms. Watson," Coral said with a tight smile. "I'll have my usual ..."

"... same thing for me," Charles interrupted, pressing against the counter beside her.

Tommie raised her eyebrows but refrained from commenting. She grabbed another jumbo teacup from the caddy and added tea ball infusers packed with *Fruity Friendship* to both cups. Then, she poured boiling water from an electric kettle into the cups and set them on plain white saucers.

Coral and Charles both laid five-dollar bills on the counter at the same time. As Tommie reached for the money, Charles grabbed Coral's teacup.

"No, Charles. That's mine, you jerk. Get your grubby hands off," Coral squawked.

"What's the difference?" he growled.

"Coral has a certain cup she prefers, Charles. Here, yours is exactly the same but a different color," Tommie explained, pushing his cup and saucer forward.

"I don't see what the big deal is. A cup's a cup. But, you go on and take your special cup, Coral. Have it your way, just like everything else," he said splashing his hot tea on the floor as he jerked the cup and saucer off the counter.

"Sorry Coral," Tommie said. "Do you want a fresh teacup? Just take a jiffy."

"No, thank you. I prefer my regular one." She walked over to the self-serve counter and added a splash of milk, a lemon wheel, and two packets of raw turbinado sugar before settling herself in her usual seat near the bookcases with a view out the windows.

Charles, in the meantime, took his teacup and saucer directly to a table at the other end of the room and sat, glaring at Coral angrily.

At 12:20, Tommie spotted Beverly Cantrell and Henry Erving sharing a sack lunch in the gazebo.

At 12:24 three more customers came in, got their tea, and visited the self-serve counter.

At 12:27, all hell broke loose.

Charles Williams left his seat and strode to Coral's table, depositing himself in the chair opposite her. He leaned forward with both hands flat on the tabletop and glowered.

"I'm warning you, Coral Beadwell. You leave me be." Tommie could hear the menace in his voice.

Coral's face was flushed bright red. She took a hiccupping gulp of air and pitched head-first to the floor.

Charles pushed away from the table in alarm, staring open-mouthed as she lay at his feet, her grey hair wet from the tea which splashed into her face on the way down, her glasses lying beside the broken teacup.

The two women customers screamed, and the man, holding a cellphone, stood frozen. "Call 9-1-1, call 9-1-1," he shouted without dialing the number.

Tommie, in an effort to get to Coral as quickly as possible, threw herself onto the floor and scrambled through the opening in the counter on her hands and knees. When she reached her, she rolled the woman on her back and began to do chest compressions.

"One little, two little, three little Indians, four little, five little, six little Indians, seven little, eight little, nine little Indians, ten little Indian children," she sang over and over until the EMTs arrived and took over.

Five minutes later, Coral Beadwell was rolled out the door on a gurney and loaded into the ambulance. The lights had been flashing, but the siren didn't sound. Tommie knew she was dead.

The traumatized patrons milled about the shop, all trying to make sense of what they had just witnessed. Tommie took up a position by the door so nobody would leave. She was sure the Floribunda Police Department would want to conduct interviews with all of them.

Tommie saw Henry Erving cleaning up the mess on the floor. There were welled tears in his eyes, and he seemed disoriented. He was about to throw the broken cup and soggy napkins into the trash, but Tommie stopped him.

"Police might need those, Henry," she said, gingerly taking the mess from him with a plastic grocery bag she kept in her pocket for cleaning up spills. She transferred the cup pieces and sodden napkins into separate zipper lock bags before setting them behind the counter. Henry nodded slowly and sat down at the table next to Charles, who was in a daze and had not moved from his seat. Beverly hovered nearby and then sat beside Henry, patting his hand sympathetically.

At 12:45, three uniformed policemen entered the shop. One of them, a young cop in his 30s, turned the sign to CLOSED, flipped the thumb lock, and then stood blocking the door. A female cop of about 40 positioned herself at the back door. The third policeman was a burly and handsome seasoned officer in his mid-to-late fifties. He walked directly to Tommie, who was standing behind the counter. Although his young partners authoritatively guarded the doors, monitoring the patrons in the room, Officer Earl Petry was clearly the person in charge.

"Hey, Ms. Watson," he said with a slight smile, his voice hushed, his steely blue-grey eyes kind.

"Hey, Earl," she responded, matching his volume level, grateful for his demeanor.

"Tommie, can you tell me what happened here?" He was tender in his approach, but he kept his intense eyes focused on her expressions as she spoke.

"Coral Beadwell came in at 12:15, ordered tea, and sat at that table over there to drink it with her lunch. Her bag and food are still on the table. At 12:27, Mr. Williams sat in front of her and seemed to be angry with her. Her face was very red, and then she just keeled over onto the floor. I got to her as soon as I could and started giving her CPR."

"You're trained in CPR, Tommie?"

"Yes. I used to be a schoolteacher. I took a course. The P.E. teacher and I were the ones designated to perform it."

"Did you see anyone try to lay their hands on Ms. Beadwell in a harmful way?"

"No. Not that I saw."

"Anybody threaten her verbally?"

"I couldn't really tell," she said, flicking a glance at Charles Williams, a look that had not gone unobserved by Earl Petry.

"Did you see anything to make you think she had been deliberately hurt?"

"No, Earl. She was just eating her lunch and drinking her tea, and then she collapsed. She's dead, isn't she?" Tommie asked, her lip quivering.

Earl lifted his eyebrows just a fraction. "I really can't say, Tommie. There's not been an announcement for the public."

"They didn't turn on the siren," she stated.

He took a deep breath and let it out slowly. "No, they didn't turn it on."

She nodded, taking her own deep breath and shifting her weight from her throbbing ankle. Earl took her elbow.

"C'mon, Tommie. Sit up here on your stool. Let me get you something to prop your leg on. There ya go. I've got to interview these other six folks. When I'm done, I'll need for you to close up shop and go on home or to the Walmart or something. OK? If there's anything suspicious about Ms. Beadwell's death ... her collapse, I mean ... your shop will have to be processed. I'm afraid you may be closed for a few days. I'm sorry about that, but it's what we might have to do."

"I understand, Earl. I do. Here's my spare key." She pressed it into his palm, and he closed his hand over her fingers for a moment, squeezing them softly before putting the key in his shirt pocket.

"Thanks. If you think of anything else later, call me. Here's my card with my number, and that's my cell number on the back. It'll be OK. Think of it as time off to rest your ankle," he said with a wink and a thoughtful smile before he went to interview the others.

Half an hour later, when all the interviews were completed, Earl locked Tommie's shop and escorted her out the back door to her car. Instead of going straight home, she had gone to her friend Annie Lang's house where she was consoled with comfort food and snacks, pampered with her feet up on a plush cushion, and distracted with three back-to-back movies from Annie's extensive collection of DVDs.

Earl texted in the middle of the third movie and asked her to meet him at the shop in the morning at 9:30. She had also received a voice message from her cousin Sanderson Harper.

"Hey, Tommie, it's Sandy. They brought Ms. Coral Beadwell in here today and the circumstances surrounding her death are suspicious. It's gonna be real important that you're truthful and cooperate with the Police. No need to call me back. Just make sure you check off all your boxes. Bye."

In light of those two messages, by the time Tommie Watson had gotten home, she barely had the strength to feed the dogs, much less wonder about whether or not the Irishman had arrived. Exhausted, but too keyed-up to sleep, she had pulled out her mortar and pestle and gone to work at the makeshift counter on her ottoman making some *Zzzzz-Tea* to help her rest. After a hot shower, the *Zzzzz-Tea* worked its magic, and Tommie Watson was able to get a good night's sleep.

Chapter Six

FINBAR HOLMES had almost completed his unit's indoor renovations by Tuesday. The honey-colored wood floor planks were glued down throughout the house, and he had installed four-inch yellow pine tongue and groove boards to the walls and ceilings in the living room, dining room, kitchen, hallway, and second bedroom. They were stained a soft buttery blond color and sealed with Tung oil, giving them a warm matte finish that complemented the flooring and instantly transformed the space into a cozy home.

Holmes installed the same boards to the master bedroom ceiling and painted them a neutral white semi-gloss to reflect the soft lighting from the bedside lamp. The walls were painted a light peach with white trim and matched the quilted bedspread made by his late wife Mary. It covered his pillow-top Queen-sized mattress and set off the new bedroom furnishings. He bought the natural oak headboard, dresser, twin night tables, and matching highboy chest online from Badcock's Furniture and had them delivered and set up by workers from the local store. Badcock's had also delivered a honey oak dinette set, along with a medium brown tweed sofa with a matching armchair for the living room, a round dark brown leather ottoman, and a large oak entertainment center, which he positioned in front of the louvered double front windows.

Other deliveries included four unassembled six-foot bookcases in flat boxes and a grey fabric futon sofa for the spare bedroom/office from Walmart, as well as a microwave, an electric teakettle, a 40-inch flat screen television, and four cases of Guinness beer in cans.

His personal items, which had been pre-shipped from Dublin, filled only three large cardboard storage boxes and consisted mostly of clothing, photographs in gold-toned frames, bedding, afghans and tea cozies crocheted by his late wife, memorabilia knick-knacks, items given him by his children and grandchildren, and Sherlock's bed and toys.

In a matter of one week, Finbar had completely renovated and furnished his new living space, all without detection by the woman living on the other side of the wall. He chuckled as he walked appraisingly throughout his home, straightening a crooked picture, adjusting the position of a dining chair, and repositioning the collection of bric-a-brac in the built-in display shelves. He ran his hands across the nubby fabric on the overstuffed living room seats and lovingly patted the delicate hand-tatted lace doilies he had placed on the arms and backs.

"Do you approve, m'darlin? It's not exact, but's near enough home to feel you here," he said to his wife's photograph on the end table. *Scíth go maith, mo ghrá.* Rest well, my love."

He touched his fingers to his lips and then to the picture, a gesture performed many times in the past eight years. Then, grabbing a cold Guinness beer from the refrigerator, he pulled his shirt off and strode outside wearing jean shorts and sandals, Sherlock on his heels. Taking up a position in the lawn chair, he drank his beer and sunned himself as he supervised the men in their sweatshirts assembling the six-foot high wooden privacy fence around the back yard.

While Finbar was working on his tan, Tommie was meeting with Earl at the shop. She had valiantly tried to conceal the dark circles beneath her eyes but ultimately gave up and just applied a tiny bit of blush to her cheeks to draw attention away from them. She sat at a table with her left leg propped on a box Earl had considerately fetched from the bulk herb storeroom.

Tommie strove to maintain a pleasant smile as she watched two latex-gloved men pore through her herbs and potions and tea things. All the house blends had been opened and their contents bagged, much to her despair. The natural remedies which Tommie had so carefully created and stored in the undercounter mini refrigerators were sitting on the counters, exposed to the warmer temperature of the ambient air, spoiling. W*ho's going to reimburse me for my product,* she wondered, *and the time it's taken to make my potions?*

All the hard surfaces in the shop were covered with smudges of black fingerprint powder. Every teacup in the caddies had been dusted for prints, and even the ones in the dishwasher had been removed and contaminated. *Those will all have to be rewashed and sanitized,* she thought, *and I'll have to spray and wipe down every single table and chair.*

Earl carefully watched her face as her eyes darted around the room. He noted her distressed expression, and he was acutely aware of her body language. Each time one of the investigating technicians touched her potions or herbs or equipment, she visibly tensed. He could see she struggled to maintain her composure, and he was impressed by her fortitude. He liked Tommie Watson a great deal. She had become a welcome addition to Floribunda in general, and Earl Petry in particular.

Earl was twice divorced, but he had no shortage of female admirers hoping to be the one to make the third time a charm. Nonetheless, he was decidedly against another marriage. He had heard through the gossip mill that Tommie was anti-marriage, too, after three failed attempts. To Earl, that was not such a deterrent, nor was her weight. He liked his women "fluffy." Age was also not a factor. She was 64; he was 58. As far as he was concerned, after the age of 45, it was all about the same. The issue was the current circumstance: Tommie Watson was officially a murder suspect.

He lifted the corners of his mouth into a smile as he regarded her. "Tommie, are you holding up all right?"

"As well as can be expected, Earl. It's all very upsetting, you know? Coral's death, this investigation …" *And people touching all my stuff,* she almost said.

"What's the most upsetting?"

"Beg pardon?"

"What's the most upsetting to you, Tommie? Coral's death?"

"Well, yes. And the fact that she died here in my shop. That's pretty traumatic. And I couldn't help her even though I tried," she admitted.

"Yes, I know you did. What else?" he prompted, hoping against hope she wouldn't say something that he would have to repeat on a witness stand.

"All this!" She swung her arm in an arc indicating the investigators. "Going through and messing with all my things!" She said it despite herself.

"I realize it's invasive," he offered.

"It's more than invasive, it's destructive. My herbs are contaminated. My tonics are ruined. Who's going to replace them? Who's going to pay for my property, my time?" she cried aloud as a tear escaped her eye and traveled down her cheek.

"Tommie, we have to be thorough. A crime was committed ..." he began.

"What crime? What crime, Earl? She collapsed. A horrible man threatened her, and it was too much for her heart. Why aren't you questioning him instead of futzing through my things?" She was angry now, and in her anger, she lashed out at the one person who was being kind to her.

Earl put his hand over hers, but she withdrew it and wiped at her teary eyes and runny nose.

"Why? Why, Earl? I'm not a suspect, but I feel like one with this treatment."

Earl sat very still for a moment, and in that moment, Tommie realized she *was* a suspect. Earl felt the tangible shift in her demeanor, and it saddened him.

"Tommie Watson," he said with a deep sigh, "I have to tell you that you are a suspect in the death of Ms. Coral Beadwell, and if you'd prefer to have an attorney present before you say anything else to me, you may."

"No." Her voice was emphatic. She blinked twice and stared in disbelief at her hands folded on the tabletop. Then, she raised her head and looked him directly in his pewter eyes.

"Earl Petry. I don't know you well, but what I do know is that you're a fair, honest man. Please, tell me right now what you think happened and why I'm a suspect." She was composed, and her voice was well modulated. She searched his face and waited for an answer.

"Coral Beadwell was murdered yesterday in your shop in the presence of seven people. It's my job to find out who, why, and how. You are only one of those seven people. You are not the only suspect. And that's about it," he said.

"Eight people."

"What?"

"There were eight people. Five in the shop, one came in just before she died, one came in afterwards, and one come in both before and after."

"Who else was here?" he asked.

"Somebody came in the back door and used the restroom at 11:55, Beverly Cantrell came in at 12:05, and she and Henry Erving both came in after the EMTs."

"So, eight people. I counted Henry and Beverly in the seven people I interviewed yesterday. Who was in the restroom?"

"I only saw her from the back, but it looked a lot like Linda Beadwell."

"Did she speak?"

"No, and I just saw her leaving out the door, so I'm not positive it was Linda."

"OK. Good to know. You're very observant. How is it you're so precise with the times?" he asked.

"Occupational hazard. I was a schoolteacher, and everything ran by the clock. And as an herbalist, I have to be exact in making my teas and potions, down to the minute. That's why the gigantic clock with a second hand on my wall."

"I'm … I'm impressed. Who knew?" He marveled at her ability to focus in the midst of chaos.

She shrugged. "I guess. You said Coral was murdered, Earl. How do you know that?"

"I can't really tell you the details, Tommie."

"Well, it wasn't a heart attack or a stroke or a brain aneurysm," she reasoned.

"It was not."

"It wasn't a physical thing. She wasn't bludgeoned or strangled or stabbed or shot or blown up with a bomb or exploded in spontaneous combustion."

"She was not." He nearly smiled but caught himself before it reached his mouth.

"That only leaves one thing. She was poisoned."

He was serious once again and sat silently.

Tommie's gaze shifted slowly around the room counterclockwise from her position in the corner near the trash bins, stopping briefly on each area as though taking a mental picture. Her eyes swept over the tables and chairs, the self-serve counter, the door to the herb storage room, the back door, the bathroom, the adjoining door to *Brewster's*, the potions prep counters and cabinets, the house blend canisters on the counter, the pickup and cash register area, the teacup caddies, the small drink coolers, the right window and display, the front door, the bookcases, the left window and display, and finally back on Earl's face. She leaned her elbows on the table and brought her clasped hands up as though in prayer, resting her chin on her laced fingers.

"I have one thing to say, Earl, and I want you to listen really well. I did not kill Coral Beadwell."

He smiled, clearly relieved. "That's what I wanted to hear."

Chapter Seven

TOMMIE WATSON got home that afternoon before dark, for a change. Zed and Red were delighted to see her and tried to tell her about the excitement outside and the strange dog they smelled, but Tommie didn't seem to understand, so they stood at the back door and whined. Since it was still daylight, and the temperature had risen to the high-60s, she grabbed their leashes from their hooks in the hallway. Red did a joyous dance on his back legs when he saw her holding them. When Zed caught the familiar scent of his leash, he whirled in circles until she trapped him between her legs and fastened it in place on his harness.

She opened the back door, and the two old dogs bolted out like they were young again. They were met by an equally excited Jack Russell Terrier. The three of them went around and around sniffing hind ends. Tommie would have been amused had it not been for what was directly in her sightline: a skinny, hairy man laid back in her blue Adirondack chair wearing nothing but short denim pants.

She let out a scream and jerked on the leashes, causing Red to yelp. Then man abruptly sat up and waved at her.

"Halloo! How're you doin', missus?" he called.

Tommie was struck mute. She stumbled backward as he rose from the chair and advanced on her.

"I'm yer neighbor. 'Tis nice to meet you at last."

It was apparent he was the Irishman who had bought the duplex. Tommie was flustered but tried not to show it. All she could think of was the unfinished welcome basket in the house as she genially shook his offered hand.

"I'm ... I'm Thomasina Watson, but people call me Tommie. Please, don't evict me," she blurted.

Finbar pursed his thin lips and raised his bushy eyebrows in surprise, and then he laughed enthusiastically.

"No, no. I'll not do it, missus. I'll be glad to have you here."

Tommie almost fainted with relief. Instead, she burst into tears, and Finbar led her to the chair.

"What's all this?" he asked. "I'm sorry to have given you a jump. Stop yer tears, lad."

"I'm sorry. It's been a bad couple of weeks. I thought for sure you'd make me move."

"Nah. I can see from your leg that you can't do

much moving. Had one like that myself years ago on m'knee. Restricts you a bit."

"Yeah. Broken ankle. It's better, but it's sure not 100 percent."

"Ah. So, tell me Thomasina-but-people-call-me-Tommie. D'you like it here?"

"I do. I really do. When Beverly said somebody bought the duplex, she told me I'd have to get out."

"Ach. She was a right git, that woman. Didn't care for her, myself. Or yer man Charlie, either."

"He's not *my* man!" Tommie exclaimed.

"It's just an expression. The pair of them can rot, for all I care."

Tommie allowed herself a slight smile.

"There, that's better. Now, let's get acquainted. My name is Holmes."

"As in Sherlock Holmes?"

"Yah, but that's *his* name, not mine," he said, jerking his thumb toward his little dog. "Mine's Finbar. It means 'fair-haired' in Gaelic. Was right descriptive when I still had a full head of it."

"Finbar Holmes. And that's Sherlock. Funny. Those are my boys, Zed and Red. Zed's the Boston Terrier, and Red's the Portuguese *Podengo Pequeño.*"

"Oh. A fancy breed, have you?"

"No, they're both rescue dogs. Zed was given away because his owners lived on a small farm and he liked to sample the chickens. Red was a stray I got from the pound. I didn't know his breed until I saw his twin on TV in a dog show. I didn't tell him he was purebred. It'd go to his head."

Finbar laughed heartily. "I like that. Sherlock is a pound dog, too. They're better if got like that, y'know?"

"Yeah, I think so, too. So, I was expecting you last Friday. When did you get here?"

"I come in on a Wednesday last in the afternoon. That woman brought me out, and Sherlock and I've been here ever since."

"Really? I had no idea. I haven't heard a sound from next door."

"That's because I've gone to bed early and been quiet whilst you've been home from work each morning and evening. I've done my work during the daytime. Would you care to come in and see? And you can have a bit of brown bread with butter 'n' cheese and a suppa tea."

He didn't wait for her answer. He strode off toward the duplex and entered his unit, leaving the door standing open.

"I'll just put the dogs in the house," she called.

"Nah. Let them off their leads. They'll not go anywhere," he responded from inside.

"No, Red's a runner. I'd lose him for sure. And Zed's basically blind, so he might wander into the street."

Finbar stepped into the doorway. He had put on sandals and a grey t-shirt that read *Find it in Florida* in big red letters. "Thomasina. Did you not see the fence?

The dogs'll not stray away. I promise."

For the first time Tommie realized what was different about the yard: it was enclosed in a high wooden privacy fence.

"When did all this happen?" she asked, regarding the fence in amazement.

"Today. Finished just before you came home. D'you like it, missus?"

"I love it!" she exclaimed as she unhooked the leashes and laid them on the chair. "I absolutely love it."

"Lovely. C'mon in and let's have a sup."

Tommie entered the back door and was instantly transported into another world. It was entirely unlike her side of the duplex, which was cold and sterile with its grey walls and brown painted concrete floor.

"Whoa! Did you do all this yourself? While I was at work? Wow. I'm impressed. It's beautiful."

"Thank you. And if your side is anything like mine was, we'll have to fix it, as well. I love working with m'hands. I used to be a decorator."

"Like an interior designer? Is that what you did in Ireland? Decorating?"

"I don't think it means the same here in America. I was married and had four children by the time I was 24. Here, sit down and I'll tell you more about myself whilst I get our tea and bread ready."

Tommie sat at the dinette with her back to the front window so she could keep an eye on the dogs outside, while Finbar fussed about the kitchen preparing the tea and bread and cheese.

"I was a fisherman from the time I turned 126 years old. I married my Mary when I was 19 and she was 17, and we lived in Dublin. I had a motorcar accident when I was just 30, and I laid up in a coma for many months. When I came awake, my knee was crushed, my shoulders was broken, and I couldn't fish anymore, so I went to school and became a decorator. In Ireland, a decorator is someone who does carpentry and painting inside residences. It was a good job. I made plenty of money to support my wife and my lads.

"You had four boys?" Tommie asked.

"No. Two boys, two girls."

"But you just called them lads."

"We calls everybody lads. Boys and girls."

"Oh. OK. Sorry to interrupt. Go on."

"When I was 50, my Mary got the cancer, so I went to school for a year and trained to be an FSAI Inspector. That's someone who does inspections for the Food Safety Authority of Ireland. They was good wages, so we used what we needed for daily living and banked the rest. Mary's treatments were paid by the government, but I took some money out to make her more comfortable at the end. She died eight years ago this April." He made the sign of the cross. "When I turned 66, I became a pensioner and now I collect my government income."

"Is that like retirement?"

"Exactly. I still get my pension, even though I live in America. I'm 71 now."

"Beverly Cantrell said you paid cash for the duplex. Is that because you banked most of your money?"

"Did she now? That's rather cheeky of her to tell my personal business."

"I'm sorry. Cheeky of me to ask, huh?" Tommie was embarrassed by her faux pas.

"No, lad. It's a fair question. I don't mind telling you. I buys everything cash. Never was one to carry any debt. Besides banking my wages, I did some investments that were profitable. And, of course, I play the ponies, and a lot of them win. If you like, I'll teach you how to pick a horse."

"Sure. I could always use some extra cash. You said earlier you were a food inspector. Does that make you 'Inspector Holmes'?" she asked with a wink and a dimpled grin.

"Suppose it does. 'Twas my title for a number of years. Not only that, I'm a great lover of puzzle solving. It's my hobby. I do sudoku and crossword, read mysteries, and watch detective films on the telly."

"Me too, only not the crosswords, but I do love to solve mysteries."

"Delightful. Maybe we can team up and outguess the telly detectives."

"That'd be fun.

"Lovely. Now, how do you take your tea, missus Thomasina? Milk or lemon?" he asked.

"Neither. I usually drink it with sugar or honey, if you don't mind."

"Oh, well, I don't have either one. I'm diabetic, so no sweets for me. I'm sorry. No, wait. I've ordered in a few times. Just let me see. Ah, yes. Will these do?" He pulled two packets of sugar from a sack in the garbage.

Tommie laughed aloud. "Why not? I've eaten from the trash can before."

"Here you are, then," he said, handing her the sugar. He poured her a steaming mug of nearly black tea from a cozy-covered teapot and set a plate down with thick slices of dense brown bread.

"Irish soda bread. I make it myself. And this is some sliced Wexford cheese I brought in my luggage and some Kerrygold butter from your *Walmart. Sláinte!*"

"*Sláinte,*" Tommie repeated. "And that means what in English?"

"Health," Finbar said. "D'you like the bread?"

"Mmm. It's wonderful. I like the butter, too, and especially the cheese. It's very strong," she said, her jaws vigorously chewing the dense bread.

"Yah. Puts hair on yer chest. You can see I've eaten more than my share."

Tommie almost spit out her bread. Finbar was hairy all over—chest, arms, back, and legs. He chortled at her reaction and continued drinking his tea.

"Yer turn, lad, if you can chew and talk at the same time. Tell me about Thomasina Watson."

"I am 64 years old. I was a schoolteacher for 20 years, but I didn't start teaching until I was 35. After I retired from the school system, I was the Education Director for a children's museum in Bay City for several years. That's about an hour or so away. I've been married a few times, and I have three children: two girls who are married and live in Tallahassee, and an unmarried son who manages a restaurant in Sugar Sands Beach. All of them are about an hour and a half from here. I worked as a technical writer for a couple of years, and then I retired at 62 and started drawing my social security while I took online courses and became a certified herbalist. I run a little shop in town called Watson's Reme-Teas where I sell herbal teas and natural remedies."

"I should like to visit your tea shop soon."

Tommie's face immediately clouded over. She had almost forgotten that her shop was closed, and she was a murder suspect.

"Missus, what's wrong?"

Her eyes teared up again, and she fought to regain control of her emotions.

"Thomasina?"

"My shop is closed indefinitely, Mr. Holmes."

"Oh? And does that have anything to do with yer tears earlier, dear?"

He was sweet and tender, and she found herself

spilling out the details of the whole story to him.

"… and now my shop is a crime scene and I am a suspect in Ms. Beadwell's murder, and if I lose my shop, I won't be able to pay my rent, and I'll have to move away and rent some less expensive shabby place or go on welfare or something like that," she blubbered, wiping her red nose and watering eyes with a napkin.

"Now, now, now. Stop yer weeping. I won't have you put out on the street. You'll stay right here in yer home. I promise you that. I own this property now, and I can charge my tenant whatever lease I desire, and I think what you pay now is too much anyways. What do you think, Sherlock?"

The dogs had heard the noise and smelled the cheese. They sat drooling at their masters' feet, their heads rotating from side to side comically. The sight made Tommie giggle.

"There, you see? The lads say for you not to worry. We'll all stay here together, and we'll be the best of friends. *Tuig?* Understand?"

"*Tuig,*" she agreed.

"Go on to yer house and get a bit of rest. Then come back over at 6:30, and we'll have a bite of supper. Do you like fish and chips? I fix a fine flaky breaded cod and fried spuds with malt, and maybe even some rissole and marrowfat peas. Would you like that?"

Tommie nodded, even though the only thing that sounded recognizable was fish.

"Lovely. And when you come back, we'll take pen and paper and begin making out a list."

"A list?"

"A list of suspects and clues. We're Inspector Holmes and Dr. Watson, are we not?"

"I suppose you're right," she snickered.

"Right, then. Go get some rest and come back soon, Watson. The game's afoot!"

Chapter Eight

FINBAR'S FISH AND CHIPS were not exactly the meal Tommie expected when she came to his unit for dinner. Instead of rectangular strips of pasty minced mystery fish baked on a sheet pan and served with a side of ketchup, what she received was a huge filet of battered and fried white cod that filled her entire plate. Chips were not potato chips at all. Finbar called those "crisps" and said they were not a meal item but a snack. The Irish version of chips consisted of long, thick wedges of russet potatoes which were expertly fried, with crispy exteriors and soft interiors.

The other two sides were presented on a smaller plate. They included rissole—a patty of compressed minced cod, mashed potatoes, herbs, and seasonings rolled in breadcrumbs and deep fried—and marrowfat peas—mature green peas which had been dried out naturally on the vines instead of being harvested young as they were in America.

Finbar placed a bottle on the table, but it was not tomato catsup; it was malt vinegar. The traditional way of eating the meal was by liberally sprinkling both the fish and the chips with coarse salt and malt. Always willing to try new things, Tommie followed suit and was amazed at the difference in taste.

"Oh my gosh. This is way better than fish sticks and French fries," she gushed.

"Good. Now, try yer rissole and mushy peas," Finbar suggested. (He pronounced them "mooshy" peas.)

Tommie took a bite of the rissole patty and declared it was the tastiest thing she had ever placed in her mouth. The peas—not so much. They were mushy, to be sure, and so starchy they stuck together in a clump on her tongue. She had to wash them down her throat with water.

"What d'you think?" Finbar asked.

"I think it's all delicious. But, quite honestly, I'm not overly fond of the peas," she admitted.

"It's an acquired taste, like black pudding. I'll fix that for you for breakfast one day."

"Black pudding? Sounds like a dessert."

"No, dear. It's more of a savory breakfast dish. Maybe tomorrow morning. The peas, though. They're marrowfat peas cooked down until their texture is soft. First, you've got to soak them in bicarbonate for an hour or more."

"Bicarbonate, as in bicarbonate of soda? Baking

soda? Why do you do that?" she asked.

"To take the farts out, of course," he replied with a wink, scooping a lumpy wad of peas onto the back of his fork with his knife.

Tommie couldn't contain her guffaw, and food exploded from her mouth, just barely caught in time by her napkin.

Though she couldn't finish her peas, she ate every morsel of the fish, chips, and rissole. Afterward, she helped him clear the table and opened the dishwasher to load, but he set the dishes in a sink of soapy water to soak. He told her he always washed by hand, but he was glad of the dishwasher as a place to let them drain. Tommie shrugged and went back to the table.

"I've got no sweets, myself being diabetic, but I can offer you a nice suppa tea. I found some more sugar packets in the waste bin," he said.

"Thank you. I'll take the tea, but I brought over some honey I can use since you can't," she said, picking up the small basket she had set down on the floor. "And here is a special tea blend I made just for you."

"You made it for me? How lovely. Let's have that later, shall we?" he said, taking the basket from her. "Oh, and a tea egg, too. Aren't you thoughtful? And some cream, as well."

"That's for your last cup of tea at night. It'll help you sleep and give you good dreams. You should probably put it in the fridge for now."

"Oh, thank you, lad. I can't wait to try it. Now, whilst we drink our tea, perhaps we can get a lead on solving this murder that's happened in yer shop, eh?"

Finbar brought a yellow legal pad and a pen to the table. Tommie could see there was writing on the pad already. After a couple of sips, he pushed his mug to the side and pulled the pad in front of him.

"All right, Thomasina. The first thing I do when I'm trying to solve mysteries on the telly is make a list of the crime, the victim, and the logical suspects."

"You do that while you're watching the movie?"

"Why, yes. How else could you solve it?"

Tommie chuckled. *He's charming, but he sure is an odd one. Best to let him take the lead since he's done it already.*

"I'll ask you questions, Thomasina, and you give me the answers. We can get this filled out in no time."

"Sounds reasonable to me. I'm ready."

At the top of the page in underlined capital letters was written: <u>CRIME: DEATH IN WATSON'S TEA SHOP</u>. Beneath that was written: <u>VICTIM:</u> Finbar began his crime-solving process with the first question.

"There can be no crime without first there being a victim, so who was the victim, missus?"

"Ms. Coral Beadwell. C-o-r-a-l B-e-a-d-w-e-l-l."

"What was the weapon?"

"Poison."

"Method?"

"You mean, how was she poisoned?"

"Yes. By what means was she poisoned?"

"I don't know that yet."

Finbar looked up and nodded thoughtfully "I will leave it blank for now. We'll come back and fill it in a bit later."

"I'm hoping I can get that information from my cousin. He's the county coroner."

"Perhaps you can put in a call to him tomorrow. That would be most helpful," he suggested.

"Sure. That'll work," she said.

"Let's continue. Date and time?"

"Monday, February 11, 2019. 12:28 p.m."

He regarded her quizzically. "How d'you know the very time she died?"

"I've got a big clock on the wall."

"Well done. Where was the victim discovered?"

"On the floor of my shop. Watson's Reme-Teas. That's R-e-m-e-dash-T-e-a-s."

"Delightful name. I very much like it, by the way. Who discovered the victim?"

"There were five of us in the shop, but I guess you'd say I discovered her since it was my shop."

"Thomasina Watson. Proprietor."

"Who was present when the victim, Ms. Beadwell, was murdered?"

"Let me see. Charles Williams. Don Lareby. Susan Clay and her sister Elaine Frank. And myself, of course. Do you need spellings?"

"Not right now. All right. Were there any other people around? Maybe outside?"

"Well, yes. Beverly Cantrell came in just before and right afterwards."

"Oh, rot. I don't care for that one. Anyone else?"

"Henry Erving was there right afterwards. Oh, and somebody snuck in my back door and was in the restroom. I didn't see her face, but from the back she looked like Coral's sister-in-law Linda Beadwell."

"How'd you happen to notice her?"

"I heard arguing from the next shop, then the door slammed, and it sounded like my back door had opened, but I didn't see anyone when I looked. Then, just after I turned my sign, I glimpsed the woman slipping out the back."

"Interesting," Homes said, making a note on his pad. "Whose shop is next door?"

"My friend Sarah Beth Brewster."

"Would that be Brewster's Coffee Shoppe? I saw it when I visited the housing agents on Wednesday last."

"Yes, it is, and my shop is right beside it."

"Lovely location, across from that little park. Now, missus, can you give me a description of the victim, Coral Beadwell? Just a sketch of what she looked like, what age, what she was wearing, that sort of thing. Slowly, please, so I can write it all down."

Tommie sat back against the chair and stared at

the ceiling, lost in the soft blond lines of the wood as she brought Coral Beadwell to mind.

"She was late 50s. I want to say 58. Think I heard that somewhere. Height I'm not so good at. Taller than me, shorter than you. Kind of right in between."

"I am 1.70 meters. You are about 1.60 meters. Let's put her in the middle at 1.65 meters."

"How tall is that in feet and inches?"

He smiled indulgently. "I do wish you Americans would adopt the metric system. That would be five feet, five inches. Weight?"

"Um, here again, I'm not so good with that. Somewhere between you and me, but a little more on the heavy side. And before you guess, I am ashamed to admit I'm 200 pounds." Her face burned, but he seemed unconcerned.

"I'm 10 stones. That's 140 pounds."

"How many stones am I?" she asked.

"Oh, about 14.2," he responded.

"Dang. I sound better in stones."

He chuckled. "Don't we all? Let's see, half of our combined weight would be 170 pounds. We'll just add 10 pounds and say 180."

"That'd make her just about 13 stones?"

"Brilliant. I think you might get the hang of it. Now, what were her facial features like? Hair? Eyes?" What was she wearing when it happened?"

"She had grey hair, and she always wore it in a

ponytail. A low flat one; not a high bouncy one. Medium blue eyes, square black frame glasses. I never saw her that she wasn't in a powder blue *UPS* shirt and khaki slacks. Wonder if she even wore that uniform to church on Sundays. Never any makeup. That's about it."

"Did the victim look any different when she came into yer shop on Monday? Pale, flushed, disheveled, made up?"

"No, except just before she collapsed, I noticed her face was really red. Could that be important?"

"It might be. It just might be. I think we should get a bit of description for the people who were in and about yer shop when Coral died. First, Charles Williams." He wrote the name in capital letters beside the number one.

"He's 49, heavyset, probably close to six feet tall, no clue about weight but he seems fit ..."

"I'd say 13½ stones, give or take a bit, from the look of him on Wednesday last."

"OK. Dark black hair, beady dark brown eyes, thin mustache, round wire-rimmed glasses. He owns Floral Real Estate and is a huge pain in the butt."

"I agree with you there. I reckoned him a right bloody arse when I met him. All right. Don Lareby?"

"Don Lareby. I'd guess early 40s, a bit shorter than Charles, slenderer, works at the First Floribunda Bank, wears suits, brown hair, light eyes like an amber color, kind of quiet. Susan Clay and Elaine Frank are his sisters."

"Tell me about the sisters."

"Susan Clay and Elaine Frank are identical twins. Mid-forties, female versions of Don in looks, your height, my weight. All three of them work at the bank together."

"They all sound rather unremarkable."

"They are, now that you mention it. They're always pleasant, but they seem more like placeholders instead of actual people—like extras in a movie, you know what I mean?"

"Excellent observation, Watson." He winked at her. "How about this Henry Irving?"

"That's Erving with an E instead of an I," she said, looking at his paper. "Henry is a quiet man, from what I can tell. He works at the UPS Store with Coral. He's early 60s, taller than Charles—I'm guessing six feet and one or two inches. Not fat but has a paunch belly. Light hair, pale eyes, ruddy complexion, wide hips, and hairy knuckles."

"That's an important detail, them hairy knuckles. I have those as well." Holmes laughed, and she blushed.

"OK. Beverly Cantrell you've met, so you tell me how you'd describe her."

"Good on you, Thomasina. Miss Beverly Cantrell, the woman who came in twice. I would describe her as being 55 or 56 years of age, judging from the fine creases in her forehead filled with cosmetics foundation. She wears quite a bit of beauty products to hide her age.

She stands five feet and eight inches—she's just above my eye level if I subtract the three-inch heels on her pumps. She is a regular dieter—one can see the horizontal lines at the edges of her mouth and the tiny vertical striations at the base of her lacquered nails. Her fingernails are professionally manicured, but her hands themselves give away her shift into menopause because of their dry and brittle skin. I detected the smell of chlorinated water beneath her bathing soap, so she likely attends a gymnasium in the mornings and showers there before she comes to work. Her dyed blond hair is naturally ash brown and is starting to grey, as evidenced by the barely grown out roots. Her eyes are pale blue but are made more tourmaline-colored with contact lenses. She is the leasing agent who works with, but is not equal with, Mr. Williams at the Floral Real Estate."

Tommie stared at him. "Dangit, Holmes! That was a brilliant deduction," she said in awe.

"Elementary, my dear Watson," he mugged.

"You watch and read too many mysteries."

"Not at all. It keeps my mind sharp. Right, Sherlock?" he said to the dog, who tilted his head in reply.

"Who's left? Ah, the one who was not officially present. Linda Beadwell. What about her?"

"I'm not going into your level of detail. Here's the *Cliff Notes* version. Linda's a social butterfly. Younger than Coral, early 50s, a bit taller than Beverly, attractive in a put-together sort of way, heavily mascaraed eyelashes and honey brown eyes, very fit. There's only one gym here, and lots of women go there. Beverly, Linda, and Sarah Beth, too. The thing about Linda that's really distinctive is her hair. It's a dark shiny walnut color with light blond highlights. And she wears it in a rounded, curled under style with short bangs and chin level on the sides and back. I think people used to call it a 'Prince Valiant' pageboy."

"Sounds ghastly."

"It is."

"How about Sarah Beth Brewster?"

"She never came into the shop."

"But she has access, does she not?"

"Yes, I guess so. Sarah Beth is 55 and very pretty, with naturally curly light auburn hair and jade green eyes. She's 5'4" tall and in great shape. I'd say she's much more fit than either Beverly or Linda. She works out at the gym every single morning before she opens her coffee shop at 6:00 a.m. I guess she's the last one."

"No, Thomasina. She is not the last suspect. You are, and I can describe you—a lovely, engaging, intelligent woman of 64 years. Slightly wavy salt and pepper hair in a pixie cut. Height 1.60 meters. Weight 14.2 stones. Olive skin tone. Bright eyes so dark brown they appear black. Deep dimples. Bow-shaped mouth with lines at the corners from frequent smiling and laughing. Small hands with strong fingers. Broken left ankle set in a walking boot. Clever and observant. Certified herbalist. Lives with two fine rescue dogs, so one can tell she is compassionate. Easily makes strangers feel like friends and brings them homemade tea blends and special milk."

Tommie was touched beyond words, and tears welled up in her eyes. In just a few hours, Finbar Holmes had become her friend, her confidant, and her partner in crime solving.

"So, missus, there it is. We have listed our suspects. Tomorrow, come over at half nine, and I'll fix you a traditional Irish Breakfast. You can ring your cousin in the morning and find out our murder method. The tea's gone cold, so I propose we have some of your special blend—and I'll have a bit of that *Dreamer Creamer* you brought over—and we'll call it a good night's work."

Chapter Nine

TOMMIE'S DREAMS were not as pleasant as she hoped Finbar's were. Her mind replayed Coral Beadwell's death over and over, and each time, it became more bizarre until she finally woke up, sweating and breathless. The last images she recalled before the dream drifted away were confusing: Coral's face glowed fire engine red as she sat drinking from an unusually large teacup the size of a mixing bowl with a handle; Charles Williams towered over her wearing a top hat like the Mad Hatter yelling, "Off with her head"; Don Lareby swayed to and fro, his arms ending in cell phones instead of hands; His identical twin sisters (dressed like Tweedle-Dee and Tweedle-Dum) stood on either side of him and spoke like a looped recording, repeating "9-1-1. What is your emergency?"; Beverly Cantrell and Henry Erving stood with their arms, faces, bodies, and bulging eyes plastered against the glass; and Linda Beadwell stood in the bathroom, dressed as Prince Valiant with a sword, stabbing at Sarah Beth

Brewster, who stood in the herb storage room and parried with her own sword.

The bedside clock read 7:45. Zed and Red were still snoring under the covers, so Tommie got on up and took a long, hot shower. Because she was unsteady and couldn't put any weight on her left foot, she had to sit on a plastic milk crate covered with a towel in the tub and direct the handheld shower wand over her body. She looked forward to the day she could finally take a proper standing shower. After drying her hair and putting on a clean set of scrubs—worn not because she fancied herself a medical professional but because they were roomy and had lots of pockets—she saw it was 8:30. Sanderson would be at work at the coroner's office.

She took a cup of Red Rooibos tea with honey to her small office, took a seat on the loveseat, and called his cell phone. Sandy picked up on the third ring.

"Sanderson Harper speaking," he said.

"Hey, Sandy. It's Tommie. I got your message on Monday. Thanks for giving me a heads up about talking to the police," she said in her brightest voice.

"Hi, Tommie. Are you all right?" he asked.

"Yes, and no. I was surprised to hear the M-word from Earl. I thought Coral had a heart attack or a stroke."

"Yeah, no. It was definitely not either of those."

"It was poison, right?"

"Oh? What makes you say poison, Tommie?" He sounded wary.

"Process of elimination. What kind of poison?"

"Now, Tommie. I'm not supposed to say. Did Earl tell you anything?"

"Not really too much. He did say he doesn't believe I had anything to do with it. But they've ransacked my shop just the same, Sandy. You should see the mess they made."

"I know, but it's necessary when there's a death like that in a place of business. We've analyzed most all of your herbs and potions and tea blends. Ah, tell me, cousin. How do you determine what you put in those herbal teas and natural remedies anyway?"

"Sandy, I'm a certified herbalist. I'm not a doctor, but I had to have extensive training and then pass rigorous tests, just like licensed medical personnel."

"Yeah, Tommie. That could be good for you, or it could be bad."

"What do you mean? Sandy, please tell me what you've found out. I need to know if any of my product was tampered with."

"Do your herbs come with any kinds of warnings or contraindications for people taking pharmaceuticals or who have existing conditions?" he asked, his tone becoming professional.

"Well, sure they do. I had to learn which herbs and combinations people with preexisting conditions like diabetes or allergies or even pregnancy should avoid, and which ones interact with prescribed medication, too. It's not just throwing a bunch of stuff together and calling it a remedy."

"Don't get your panties in a wad, cousin. I'm just asking a simple question."

"Well, a lot of people think I'm a witch or a quack or somebody trying to be Claire Fraser from *Outlander*. I've worked hard to learn how to use natural ingredients safely."

"What do you know about cyanide?" he asked.

"Wait, what? Cyanide? Oh my gosh, Sandy! I don't have any use at all for cyanide. Is that what poisoned Coral? Cyanide?" she asked.

"I didn't tell you that. Preliminary findings indicate that type of poison, but it'll take a while before we have the full toxicology results. Tell me about that *Fruity Friendship* tea of yours. How did you come up with it?"

"It's a base of Honeybush, which comes from Africa. It's a naturally sweet herbal tea. And then, to spice it up, I added chopped dehydrated peaches, cherries, and apricots, and some broken bits of whole cinnamon. That's all that's in it," she explained.

"Where did you get the ingredients, Tommie? Did you prepare them yourself?"

"No, I have distributors I order from. They're all very reputable, though. I've vetted them for quality control. I'm meticulous about my products. Are you saying something was wrong with the tea or the fruit in that special blend?"

"Not necessarily, but did you realize there's cyanide in apricot kernels, peach pits, and cherry rocks? If they got ground up and blended into your tea, it could be toxic for whoever drank it."

"There were no kernels, pits, or rocks in my blend. I check everything really well. Dried whole fruit. Nothing more. Even if there were, I outsource those things. I don't do the actual dehydrating. And, besides, I would have felt the hard pieces when I chopped them up," She was getting agitated.

"Tommie, settle down. Nobody's said that's where the cyanide came from. I've been covering all the bases ... for you, Tommie ... just to be extra sure you're not implicated."

"Implicated? Oh my gosh! I have absolutely *no motive* for harming Coral Beadwell. She swung business my way, for crying out loud. She was one of my best repeat customers," she said, her voice rising.

"I understand that. Relax. Your loose tea blend was cleared. The tea in the cup? Now, that's a different story. It was most definitely contaminated. It's a good thing you protected the evidence by putting the cup in a zipper lock bag. And the napkins had a cyanide-like contaminate on them, too. I hope you wore gloves when you handled them."

"No, I used a plastic bag from my pocket."

"That's a good thing, because just touching that

much cyanide can make you really sick."

"Sick, like how?"

"Dizziness, weakness, vomiting, headache, problems with your heart and breathing. Those kinds of sick. And before you ask, touching it with the plastic bag protected you from getting it in your system. What made you think to do that?"

"You and I used to play detective when we were young, remember? Plus, I didn't want to get cut by the ceramic cup shards. That's why I keep a bag in my pocket, just in case a customer spills something or breaks a cup."

"Glad you thought of it."

"Would touching it directly kill you?"

"Probably not. Just make you really sick."

"That's good to know. The teacup and the napkins. So, the brewed tea had the poison?"

"The napkins held pretty good trace from the liquid, but they were secondary to the primary source. The teacup was loaded with it, mostly on the bottom and around the rim. It wasn't the tea, Tommie; it was the cup. The cup was tainted."

Chapter Ten

"CYANIDE POISONING," Finbar said, "in and on the teacup itself. That's a new one for me."

"You and me both," Tommie agreed.

"Well, missus. This is becoming a most interesting murder case. Let me get the breakfast on the table, and we can discuss it whilst we eat."

Finbar set several serving bowls on the table, along with the cozy-covered teapot. "Help yerself," he said as he poured her a mug of the strong tea he brought over in his luggage from Dublin. Tommie stirred in the *Honey-Honey* she made (since his diabetes prevented him from using the sweetener) and surveyed the food in the assembled bowls as Finbar identified them.

"This is a traditional full Irish breakfast. These here are crispy bacon rashers, fried eggs, mushrooms, and grilled tomatoes," he said, pointing to each bowl.

"I recognize those, and that's more of the Irish soda bread and Kerrygold butter we had yesterday. And are those baked beans? For breakfast?" she asked.

"Oh yes. That's a favorite."

"That one looks like a potato pancake in the shape of a four-leaf clover."

"Hm. Never thought of it that way, but yes, it's a fried potato *farl,* which comes from the Gaelic word *fardel* meaning four parts. Well thought out, missus."

"That leaves that brown one and that black one."

"Right. The brown one is rissole hash, made from the leftover rissole we had last night. The small black patties are *drisheen*—black pudding."

"Ah yes, the black pudding you were telling me about. What's in it?"

"Protein, herbs, spices, onions, and barley. Try a bit. I like mine with tomato catsup." He served her two crispy fried black discs and a healthy squirt of ketchup.

"Oh, that's good. It has a spicy, kind of gamey taste, like sausage."

"D'you like it?"

"I do. I'll have another one, and I'll help myself to a little bit of everything else, except the tomatoes. I'm not so crazy about them."

"Are you not? But you like the tomato catsup?"

"Yeah. I don't know why. Just a preference. OK. I'm digging in." And she did. In fact, though she thought there was more food than anyone could possibly eat, she finished off her whole plate, as well as two more black pudding rounds and another spoonful of rissole hash.

When she pushed away from the table, she was stuffed.

"I need a nap now," she lamented.

"Ah! Another sup of tea should wake you up. Just leave the bowls and go sit on the sofa. I'll be right there."

Tommie waddled over to the couch and sat. She noticed it was brand new, but the doilies were much older.

"Mary made them doilies. She was good with her hands. All the furniture is new from the *Badcock's* store. Had it delivered last week," he called from the kitchen as he put plates in the sink to soak, covered bowls, and stored them in the fridge.

When he came into the living room, he pulled the top off the round ottoman, brought out a crocheted afghan, and laid it on the cushion opposite where Tommie was sitting.

"Put your legs up on this, missus, and lean back against the sofa pillow."

"Oh, no, Finbar. I don't want to get your blanket dirty," she protested.

"Jayze, Woman, I've had four children and twice again as many grandchildren. D'you think it's never had feet on it?"

She gave in, not reluctantly, and instantly felt more comfortable. He even brought out a little low tray on which she could perch her mug.

"So, I'm glad you liked the breakfast. I don't eat that way every day, but I felt we needed it this morning." He smiled.

"Why do they call it 'black pudding' instead of sausage. It was sausage, wasn't it?"

"Er, well, yes. I suppose because it's a bit gelatinous when they first combine the ingredients."

"What was the protein ... pork?"

"Yes. Yes, it was pork, sure. It came from the pig. Pig's blood."

"What? Not the meat, but the blood?"

"Don't you go getting queasy on us, now. It's pork protein, just the same."

"Well, I've eaten a lot of different things, like goat testicles in Africa. I have to say the black pudding was way better. I'll eat it again," she said with a wink.

"Good on you, Tommie. Always approach food with an open mind. I'll feed you all sorts of delicious things, like crumpets, kippers, haggis, jolly boys, deviled kidneys, tattie scones, bannocks, kedgeree, laver bread, cockles, Crempog, and bubble and squeak, just to name a few." He grinned.

"Super. Just not today, OK? Let's talk about cyanide poisoning. What do you know about it?"

"It's deadly. I'm just looking at the internet right now on my phone. Chronic symptoms—that's exposure over a long period of time—are weakness, dizziness, paralysis, liver and kidneys damage. Acute symptoms indicate a large dose of the poison and can be seizures, breathing difficulties, coma, and cardiac arrest. Says here that victims may have a cherry red face as pulmonary edema sets in. Yer Ms. Beadwell had a red face, didn't you tell me?"

"I did. And when she went over, it was like a heart attack. How is it administered?"

"It occurs in pesticides, tobacco smoke, seeds and kernels of apricots, apples, oranges, cherries, and peaches, in raw almonds, cassava, bamboo shoots, and even flaxseeds."

"We're exposed to a lot of those things all the time. I would think it'd take a highly concentrated dose, not just a few shavings from kernels and pits. Anyway, Sanderson said my tea blend was cleared. Anybody in the food service industry could have access to those food items, and so can anyone who buys groceries," Tommie contemplated with a frown.

"Tobacco smoke is implausible, wouldn't you say?" Finbar noted.

"Yeah. Gardeners use pesticides, and so do people who like to take care of their lawns, or even farmers. I feel like we're making our potential suspect pool larger instead of pinpointing anyone. Does it show anything else?"

"Hm. It says here there are traces in acetone nail polish remover."

"Like what they use at nail salons? That means someone who has their fingernails done could possibly get ahold of some, don't you think?" she asked.

"I see where you're going. Beverly Cantrell has

those professionally manicured fingernails," he said.

"Yes, she does," Tommie agreed.

"It says that cyanide salts are used when cleaning metal and doing electroplating. There are also some medications that contain cyanide: hydroxocobalamin, sodium nitroprusside, citalopram, and cimetidine. I'm not sure what those are used for. Does anyone have access to a jeweler or a chemist?"

"I don't know, but we need to find out. Where are we on our list?"

"We have a short list of suspects, and I'm going to officially discount yer name because we know you did not do it. What we don't have is motive, Thomasina. *Why* did someone want to kill Ms. Coral Beadwell. That's probably the single most important key to solving this crime. To find out motive, we must do some investigative work, and we must be careful not to alienate the *Gardai.*"

"The what?"

"The law authorities."

"Ah, yeah. How do you propose we go about our clandestine investigating?"

"We need to interview our suspects without them knowing that we are investigating them. D'you have any ideas how that can be done?"

Tommie sat upright, a huge grin making her eyes squint and deepening her dimples.

"We come a'calling. Finbar Holmes, I think it's

time for me to introduce you to the citizens of Floribunda, Florida. Meet me at my carport in twenty minutes, and we'll take a ride around the town."

Chapter Eleven

BREWSTER'S COFFEE SHOPPE was the duo's first stop. As Tommie parked the car parallel to the curb, Finbar studied the window displays in front of the store. They were orderly and attractive, if a bit pedantic in their synchronicity, with coffee packages, mugs, pots, and artificial flowers arranged in perfect alignment with one another in each window. *This is a woman who thrives on organization and control,* he speculated. He opened his door and went around to Tommie's, helping her from the vehicle, and then they entered the door.

A *ding-dong* doorbell sound caught Sarah Beth's attention. Seeing Tommie, she rushed around from behind the counter and met her in an embrace.

"I've been so worried about you, Tommie. There's all sorts of talk going around, like your tea was contaminated, your cups and equipment weren't sanitized, that you weren't really certified to make natural remedies. I told them to take their business elsewhere, if that's what they thought. Come on in and sit down. Tell me all about it," she gushed, taking Tommie's elbow and ushering her to a table.

Finbar watched the exchange with interest, hanging back until Tommie craned her head around to look for him. She motioned him over.

"Sarah Beth, I want you to meet my new friend, Inspector Holmes," she said.

Sarah Beth regarded the little man with surprise. "I'm so sorry. I thought you were here for a coffee. You're with Tommie? Did she say your name is Inspector Holmes … as in Sherlock Holmes, the detective?"

"Yes, but my name is Finbar. Sherlock is my dog. I was an inspector for the Food Safety Authority of Ireland, but now I'm just a pensioner living in Florida," he said with a smile.

"Oh! But you're Irish!" Sarah Beth exclaimed. "Are you the man who bought Tommie's duplex? You *are* going to let her stay in it, aren't you?"

"I'm himself! But, why d'you assume I would put her out? What d'you Americans think of us Irish, that we're cold-hearted like the English?" He was joking, but Sarah Beth's expression was aghast. "Woman, I'm pulling yer toes. Missus Thomasina will stay as long as she likes." He sat in a chair across the table from Tommie. When he tried to scoot it closer to the table, he noticed it was affixed to the wall with screws, rendering it immovable;

Tommie's chair was free standing.

Sarah Beth gave a self-conscious giggle and recovered from her shock. "Can I bring you both something? A latte, maybe? I don't have tea, of course."

"I'd love a glass of water, if you don't mind. Finbar?" Tommie prompted.

"I'll have a coffee with cream, please," he replied.

Tommie looked at him in surprise. "You drink coffee as well as tea?" she asked.

"And I drink water, too, but I prefer Guinness. Why d'you look so surprised?"

"Sarah Beth says 'coffee drinkers are not tea drinkers and vice versa.' That's why I'm surprised."

"Yer friend is mistaken in her assumptions."

About that time, Sarah Beth returned with the drinks, along with a fresh coffee for herself. She pulled up a nearby (unscrewed) chair from the adjacent table and sat beside Tommie.

"So, what happened over there?" she asked.

"Coral Beadwell dropped dead, right in front of me. Charles Williams was sitting at the table with her. I think he was threatening her. I heard him tell her to leave him alone or she'd be sorry. Something like that, anyway," Tommie said.

"That's terrible. I had to close up early to get groceries from Winn Dixie for dinner. If I had waited a little longer, I might've been over there to help. As it was, I had to chase Linda Beadwell out of my shop so I could leave," Sarah Beth said.

"I heard arguing through the wall. Was that you and Linda?" Tommie asked.

"Oh, yes. Afraid so. She usually comes in at 6:00 on the dot when I first open, but I had an upset stomach, so I was late getting to work on Monday morning, and my regular early crowd was a little less than usual. She must not have waited because she wasn't there when I unlocked my door."

"What was the argument about?"

"She was ticked off that I was late. Said it disrupted her whole day. I told her I was sorry, but things happen, you know? There are other places she can get coffee, but she is at my door at 6:00 on the dot every single day, like it's a ritual or something like that."

"Why was she over here at your shop so close to noon, Sarah Beth?"

"She knows I don't have much business after 10:00, just like now, and there wouldn't be anybody around to hear her cuss me out. She's getting more like Charles all the time."

Tommie shifted in her seat. "Charles? Why would you mention him?" she asked.

Sarah Beth sat back against her chair uneasily. Finbar watched the exchange with interest, letting Tommie control the conversation as he observed Sarah Beth's body language.

"Well, because ... because of their affair," Sarah

Beth said in exasperation.

"What? Affair? Charles Williams and Linda Beadwell are having an affair? Gross! I think I'll be sick!" Tommie made a gagging sound. "How do you know that, Sarah Beth?"

Sarah Beth leaned in again and took a swallow of her coffee. "For the past several months ... at least as long as you've been here in town ... they've both been coming in every morning. They stand in the order line together. Sometimes he's in front, and sometimes she is, and they stand really close together. A few times, I've even seen them bump each other, like it's accidental. But you know Charles. He takes an unintentional casual slight as a personal affront. But never once has he even hinted at being offended when Linda shoves against him. After they get their orders, they sit on opposite sides of the tables in facing chairs. You know what I mean? Like Mr. Holmes is in the wall chair, but you're in the floor chair across from him, only they put all the other tables in the row between. I've seen their eyes meet, and you can tell they have a secret thing they're hiding," she said.

"You're quite the observer, lad. Good on you," Finbar said. "You've a keen eye for detail." He smiled appreciatively and mimed tipping his hat.

"Thank you. I like to know what's going on around me. You'd be surprised what I can see from that coffee counter," she said.

"This Mrs. Beadwell ... Linda. You sent her off

when you closed up shop?"

"I did. It was just before noon, and I told her she had to go so I could get to the grocery store."

"And she left out the front or the back?"

"The back. I had already locked the front door. Tommie and I park out back. I should probably put a bell on the back door, too. I don't like for other people to come in that door because I don't notice them right away. In fact, Linda scared the crap out of me when I turned around from the cash register. She left the same way."

"So, it *was* her that came in my shop on Monday, then," Tommie said.

"She came in *your* shop? Whatever for? She's a coffee drinker, and so is Charles," Sarah Beth said.

"She came in and used my restroom, just like it was her own personal bathroom. And then she snuck out before I opened up. Never said a word. And, you're right. Charles ordered tea, but he never drank it," Tommie said.

"Maybe Linda was looking for Charles? Maybe they were in it together. Come to think of it, I saw Charles bickering with Coral Beadwell in front of the real estate office. That's another reason I rushed Linda out. I didn't want to be here in case he came over. It's all I can do not to dowse him with scalding hot coffee."

Finbar raised his eyebrows and blinked a couple of times. "He bothers you, lad?" he asked.

"He bothers both of us," she said. "He harasses us at least two or three times a week."

"That's true. He wants us to give up our leases so he can buy our shops and combine them into one for more money. He's always making allegations and complaints," Tommie said.

"I knew he was a nasty sot when I first met him. Rally up, lads. I'll see to it that Mr. Williams never takes your establishments if I have to buy them myself," Finbar said. Tommie could tell he was angry. His mouth was compressed into a line, and his large half-moon shaped ears had taken on a dark red hue.

"Well, I think we'll just slip into my shop from the side door. I know I'm not supposed to go back in there until Earl gives me the all clear, but I need to check that everything's OK. Hopefully, they didn't leave the cooler doors open and ruin *all* my product. Please don't let anybody know, Sarah Beth. Thanks so much," Tommie said, awkwardly getting to her feet.

"Yes, lad. It was my pleasure to meet you. I'm glad Thomasina has a good friend to look out for her," Finbar said, laying a few bills on the table.

"Oh, no. There's no charge for your coffee," Sarah Beth objected. "Tommie … and now you … are my friends."

"No, no. I always leave money when services have been rendered. Think of it as a gift then, Mrs. Brewster, for being Thomasina's friend. Thank you again," he said, following Tommie through the adjoining door.

Chapter Twelve

WATSON'S REME-TEAS had a reversed counter and layout nearly identical to Brewster's Coffee Shoppe, but it had an entirely different feel altogether. After years as an inspector for the Food Safety Authority of Ireland, Finbar looked at food and beverage establishments with a practiced eye for details. He could readily see past the smudges of fingerprint powder and out-of-place herb canisters and equipment and appreciate both the layout and the decorations.

People tend to eat and drink first with their eyes, so Finbar appreciated the appealing ambiance of Watson's Reme-Teas over Brewster's Coffee Shoppe. Where Sarah Beth's narrow 20-foot by 50-foot shop had a sterile feeling with its blue, grey, and gold color scheme and linear arrangement of tables and chairs, Tommie's shop, at only four feet wider, felt decidedly roomier, with a homey warmth and soothing color scheme. *More pleasing to the eye; more pleasing to the palate.*

Looking in from the doorway, *Brewster's* seating on the left side of the shop consisted of ten painted chairs in a marigold hue which were screwed to the wall opposite ten rectangular 1½-foot by 2-foot tables. These were covered with marigold and navy checkered vinyl tablecloths. Ten identical free-standing chairs sat at their ends. There were exactly two feet between each table and chair setup. A pair of identical navy-blue exterior doors with windows faced each other at either end of the store, with a three-foot walking area in between. A long U-shaped counter covered in baby blue laminate, eight feet wide by 20 feet in length, took up the right side of the shop and opened just next to the adjoining door. Along the common wall with Tommie's shop, directly behind and to the left of Brewster's display window, were three dark grey bookshelves which held retail merchandise, and to their right was a narrow self-serve counter backed up to the window display area. The flooring was grey, as were the walls. The shop appeared exactly like the window displays—orderly, attractive, pedantic, and synchronized in perfect alignment throughout.

In contrast, Finbar noted that Watson's had round tables which were two feet in diameter, with short fabric tablecloths in a rich blue-green teal color. He ran his hand across a tablecloth and could tell from the feel that the fabrics had been treated with a water repellant, making them easy to clean without having the cheap texture of the vinyl or taking away from the aesthetics of the cloth toppers.

The chairs were wood with a dark chestnut brown stain. They were arranged four to a table and formed an X-shape in a row of four seating areas grouped along the far wall, with a parallel row of three table groupings in the center of the space, allowing for 28 people to sit comfortably and maneuver between tables with ease. Even though the walls and floor were the same grey as *Brewster's,* the addition of the teal accents and natural cork hard surfaces gave a cozier feeling.

Sweeping his eyes around the shop, he could see the front and back doors were painted teal and were the same shotgun configuration, with a walkway that separated the tables from the counter. Tommie's countertops were a natural-looking cork laminate, and whereas Brewster's opened at the back end of the long U, Webster's opened in the center, and she had wooden cabinets above the counter on the common wall. Two induction cooktops were set up at the end near the adjoining door, and a glass partition insured against accidental burns by someone walking next to them.

A four-foot marble slab graced the countertop opposite the tables and was also protected by a plexiglass sneeze guard, allowing patrons to view Tommie preparing her remedies without touching or contaminating the area, much like on a buffet line. Dark amber glass tea canisters were set up on the counter on the other side of the central opening. The dark jars protected the delicate herbs from breaking down in the sun or being sullied by people touching them, and only Tommie dispensed the tea blends.

The common wall counter contained electric teakettles, teacup caddies, and disposable cups. Beneath the counter were three 24-inch refrigerators that held her perishable tonics and remedies. A double sink and dishwasher finished out the area and backed up to the sink and dishwasher in Brewster's.

At the far end of the shop, on the left, was a handicap restroom with a wooden pocket door, and opposite the bathroom on the other side of the back door, was an 8-foot by 12-foot walk-in cooler and herb storage area. A double refrigerator with a bottom freezer held perishable potions and items like cream and foodstuffs. Stainless steel floor-to-ceiling shelves on either side held boxes and jars of dried herbs, non-perishable sweeteners, and other equipment. Brewster's had a mirror image layout, except Sarah Beth's storage area was eight feet by eight feet. A self-serve counter with underneath trash bins ran the length of Tommie's storage room and completed the furnishings.

Finbar finished his survey of Tommie's shop and took a seat at the first table on the left in a chair facing toward the windows, away from the far wall. He watched as Tommie hobbled around behind the counter area, inspecting her equipment and clucking her tongue at the huge mess she encountered, but being very careful not to

touch anything.

"Yer shop is lovely, missus. I'm sorry they made such a ruin of it, but as soon as they let you back in, I'll help you set it to rights."

"Thank you, Finbar. I appreciate that more than you can imagine. I'll just be a couple more minutes. That's where Coral was sitting," she said, indicating the front left chair at the right-hand front table, "and that's where Charles was sitting before he came over to her." She pointed to the back-left chair at the far-left table near the wall, behind where Finbar sat. Holmes followed her hand and noted each position, visualizing the route the man took to get to the front table.

"And where were you, missus?"

"I was over here at the counter by the cash register. I had just served the sisters at the pick-up area. They sat with Don at your table. When Coral went down, I dropped to the floor and crawled—I can move faster that way—and came around the counter. It couldn't have taken me more than a minute, but I'm pretty sure she was dead when I was doing CPR."

"What did the other patrons do?"

"The sisters screamed, but they didn't leave their chairs. Don stood up—he was sitting where you are now—but he didn't move anywhere. Charles stayed in his seat. I don't know who called 9-1-1. One of the sisters, I think. When the EMTs arrived, I remember Henry Erving standing over there at the bookcases by the front display window."

"And Miss Cantrell?"

"She had been eating lunch in the gazebo with Henry, but I remember seeing her afterward. I think she came over when Henry did."

Holmes got up and walked to the door, looking out its window. From there, he could clearly see the gazebo, the real estate office, and the *UPS Store*. He turned to Tommie.

"And where were you when you saw the woman who came out of the loo?"

"The who?"

"The loo. The toilet."

"Oh. I was on my butt trying to scoot out of that window display by the bookcases. I had just stood up and unlocked the front door when I heard a noise, and there she was, slipping out the back door."

Finbar backed up against the raised display and tried to approximate her vantage point.

"Right, then. Shall we go do some more investigating? Who shall we interview now?"

"Let's meet Henry Erving, and then we can walk on over to Floral Real Estate and have a talk with Charles and Beverly."

"Lovely. And I can tell them you no longer need their housing services," he said with a broad grin.

Chapter Thirteen

HENRY ERVING looked up listlessly when Tommie and Finbar entered the UPS Store. To Tommie's eye, he appeared to still be in shock over witnessing Coral Beadwell's death. When they spoke with him at the front counter, he was fidgety, breathing heavily, ill at ease, and looked green around the gills, but he readily answered their questions.

"Hi, Henry. Are you doing all right?" Tommie asked with a bright smile.

"Don't feel great. As well as can be expected, I suppose, after seeing somebody I know lying dead on the floor right in front of me. I've never seen a dead body before," he lamented.

"I know. Me neither. Henry, I want you to meet my new friend, Inspector Holmes. He's moved here from Dublin, Ireland and owns the duplex I live in on Camelia, so I guess I can say he's my landlord, too."

Henry reached his arm forward and shook hands feebly. Finbar noticed his palm was sweaty.

"Nice to meet you. Hey, are you that famous Inspector from England?"

"Nah, I'm a food inspector from Ireland," Finbar said with a grin, "or at least I was until I became a pensioner and moved to Florida."

"Not Sherlock, then. I'm sorry, but what did you say your first name was again? I've been a little out of it since Monday."

"It's Finbar. It means fair-haired."

"Ah, that's interesting. What made you decide to live here, Finbar Holmes?"

"I like the sunshine. We don't see it so very often in Ireland. They don't call it the Emerald Isle because of the sun. We've a great deal of rain. I decided to move to a warmer climate in my old age. California, Florida, Canary Islands. I like a place with a beach within driving distance. I Googled and found the name Floribunda, and I liked it, so here I am," Finbar said amiably.

"That's … that's great. I've lived here all my life. But to me, it's just a place. Not a bad little town, though … most of the time. I've never met anyone from Ireland. We don't get all that many visitors from other countries."

"Pity. It's such a lovely part of the states."

"Usually. When people aren't dropping dead," Henry said, dissolving into dejection.

"Henry, you know what? My mind is so boggled

with what happened the other day. It's like I was in a dream or something. Maybe you can help me remember what went on," Tommie said.

"I know what you mean. I didn't see much," he responded with a shrug of his stooped shoulders.

"I remember seeing you eating in the gazebo with Beverly Cantrell on Monday just before Coral and Charles came in," Tommie prompted

"Yes, Bev and I had made a date to have lunch there because the weather has been so nice."

"Why, Henry," she remarked, "I didn't even know you and Beverly were dating."

"Oh, well, sure. It hasn't been long, but yeah."

"And you and Coral, were you very good friends with her?" Tommie asked with a sympathetic expression.

"Um, I guess so. We just worked together, you know? Not much more than just colleagues." He shifted from foot to foot, reluctant to talk anymore.

Finbar took over. "Ms. Watson tried to tell me about the tragedy, but she's awfully confused, poor woman. What the devil happened on Monday, Mr. Erving? D'you have any idea how yer coworker would be killed or why?" he asked.

"How would I know? I was eating lunch in the gazebo, like I said, with my girlfriend. I saw Coral and Charles walking to *Watson's* together, and they went in to the shop together."

"Would that be Mr. Charles Williams from next

door at the housing agency? He and yer lady friend were together?" Finbar asked.

"Yeah, him. I guess they've been seeing each other. I don't know. Not my business what she did with her spare time or who she carried on with. Anyway, I was with Bev when Coral died. We came over when the EMTs pulled up to see what was happening." His tone was belligerent. "I wasn't anywhere near her all day."

"Henry was kind enough to try and clean up her spilled tea and broken cup," Tommie offered.

"That's a good lad. You must've liked yer Ms. Beadwell well enough."

"I liked her fine, but we weren't dating. I went to the gazebo because the weather was nice. That's all. I wasn't stalking her or anything like that. We just worked together," Henry insisted.

"Sure. Sure. I understand. How long had you worked together?" Finbar asked.

"I started working here in 2009. Coral came on the job about 2012."

"And I suppose you were her supervisor?"

Henry was quiet a moment, clenching his teeth. A muscle throbbed at his jawline. "No, she was mine."

"She was? D'you mean they promoted her over you? That's a load of rubbish, and you having worked here longer. That would make my teeth grind. Surely you had more experience and seniority," Finbar goaded, clucking his tongue.

"I wasn't too happy about it; I can tell you that. And Coral could be a bully sometimes ... a lot of the time. That's how she got the promotion over me. She pushed her way into it. I'm more capable than she ever was," Henry retorted.

"Sure. Sure. I can tell yer a smart and capable man. Women can be that way," he said in a hushed voice. Tommie ambled around the store and pretended not to hear, letting Holmes take the lead with Henry.

"Yes, they are. I don't know what I ever saw in Coral, to tell you the truth. She wasn't nice to me at all."

"Tried to emasculate you, did she? I've seen that with women bosses. They get you interested and then dash you down without a care about yer feelings."

"You're exactly right, Mr. Holmes. I gave her a Christmas gift at the annual party this year, and do you know what she did? She threw it in the garbage and laughed at me in front of the other employees. She could be a spiteful, wicked witch."

"Without a doubt. Yer right lucky to have gotten together with Miss Cantrell. She's much better for a lad like you. And, d'you have the manager position you deserved now?"

"I do. And Bev's a great girlfriend," he said.

"Yes, I'm sure she is. She's well put together. Was she friendly with Mrs. Beadwell?"

"I don't think they had any problems, except Bev's been nice to me, and Coral made fun of her behind her back."

"That doesn't seem very sporting of her. Did she not get on well with others?"

"She was difficult. She was a lot nicer to Bev than she was to Charles, though. I thought she despised him, and it seemed like the feeling was mutual, but then she goes and meets him for lunch on Monday. I just don't get it," Henry said, looking miserable.

"Right. Well, sorry to make a short visit, but Ms. Watson is showing me about town, and I'm on her schedule. We must meet at a local pub for a pint one of these days, but first, maybe you should see a doctor. You seem *tinn go leor*—Quite unwell," Holmes said, ushering Tommie out the door.

"Boy, did you ever get him talking!" she said.

"If you know what buttons to push, you'll always get a prize. That one has more to reveal that can only be got with loads of strong drink. I'll have a go at him in on Saturday, if he's recovered. Shall we now visit the real estate ogre and his ogrette partner?" he asked.

"You bet," she said, and they walked next door.

Chapter Fourteen

FLORAL REAL ESTATE served the entire county of Floral, which included Floribunda, Cottonton, Cypress City, and Greenleaf. As the sole owner, Charles Williams received the commissions for all the properties sold by the office, regardless of which agent made the deal. He collected the full amount of the commissions and paid the agents a fixed percentage. Charles himself handled all the commercial listings, and Beverly Cantrell handled the property management leases. At present, there were no additional agents in Floribunda, but he retained an agent in each of the other offices in Cottonton, Cypress City, and Greenleaf.

The gossip through the tea-vine was that Charles was a player, and Beverly had been one of his interests at one time. Their relationship was over, but her status as second-in-command at the real estate office was somehow quite secure. As it happened, they were both in the office when Finbar and Tommie arrived.

Charles hurried to shake Finbar's hand and offered him coffee, but Holmes declined. He settled Tommie into a chair and took one himself. Beverly perched on the edge of another chair, and Charles leaned against the front desk.

"Welcome, Mr. Holmes," Charles said. "I'm glad to see you're getting out and about in our little town. Ms. Watson, it's so considerate of you to drive him."

"Yes, she's quite the peach," Holmes said. "I wanted to come by, Charlie, and tell you that I'm very pleased with the property on Camelia Street."

"I knew you would be," Beverly said. "I told Charles it was perfect for you, and you know, if you enclosed that front porch area and put a cased opening between the dining rooms, it would make a nice four-bedroom two-bathroom house."

"No, I'll not be doing that. I like Ms. Watson well enough, but we don't want to share housing quarters, not being a romantic couple, you understand."

"Ah … oh … I didn't mean. Well, I just thought that you might want to … I seem to have misunderstood," she stammered, her face flushing.

"Jeez, Beverly. Just shut up," Charles growled. "I'm sorry, Mr. Holmes. I don't know what she was thinking. She tends to run off at the mouth sometimes."

"Not at all, Charlie. It's quite understandable. I've decided that the one side is more than adequate for myself and Sherlock, now that I've finished making the necessary interior improvements to bring it up to standards. Ms. Watson shall stay in her own unit, and I will have improvements done for her as well to make her part of the home more livable."

It was Charles' turn to flush. "More livable, huh? I see. Well, this is an historical town, and many of the homes are older. We can't make *improvements* for all our renters. It's nice that you were able to buy the property and can have them done," he said.

"Thank you. Ms. Watson's situation, with her tea shop in limbo, was a factor in letting her keep her home," Finbar said.

"Oh, really? That's really quite hospitable of you, Mr. Holmes," Beverly said. "Would you like me to draw up a leasing agreement for the two of you? I have a standard form that would work. While you're both here, you can go ahead and sign it. We will be glad to manage the details," Beverly offered, getting up from her chair and teetering on her heels to the file cabinet behind the desk of the front office.

"That won't be necessary, Miss Cantrell. I can make up a Tenancy Agreement for Ms. Watson to sign once we agree on the terms. But, thank you for offering. That's very kind of you," Finbar said.

"Well, congratulations Ms. Watson. I guess now you won't be needing any of the fine rentals that I was keeping off the market for you," Beverly said. The temperature in the room seemed to drop ten degrees.

"No, but thank you anyway," Tommie said.

"By the way, Charlie. I understand you were in the tea shop when that dreadful business happened with the woman," Finbar said to Charles.

Charles regarded him, opening his little beady eyes as wide as he could manage. "Yes, I was there. It was a terrible thing. I told you this is an old town. I'm afraid the dishwasher in that shop is probably not as updated as it should be. When so many people are spreading their germs around on cups, there's bound to be sickness."

Tommie was silent, fuming at the insult, but smart enough not to take the bait. She let him blather on.

"And then, forgive me Ms. Watson, but nobody can really be sure what's in those herbs you make the tea from. I'm a coffee drinker. It's hard to mess up a drink made from coffee beans unless you use sour milk. Am I right, Mr. Holmes?" Charles said with a sneer.

"I can't really say I agree, Charlie. I hear there are people who drink an insanely expensive coffee called *kopi luwak* that's made from coffee beans which have gone through the intestinal tracks of Asian palm civets. They say it's a delicacy. I say, 'rubbish.' I'll not drink coffee that's come from an animal's arse! How about you?" Holmes asked.

Charles grimaced and pulled at his thin mustache, a distasteful expression on his face.

"I'm curious, Charlie. You say you're a coffee man, yet you were having tea in Watson's with Ms.

Beadwell," Holmes said. "Was there a friendship or a romantic relationship there?" He winked and gave Charles a leering grin.

"No!" Charles exclaimed. "I have no relationship at all with Mrs. Beadwell."

"With *Ms.* Beadwell, you mean?" Holmes asked. "Ms. Coral Beadwell."

"That's what I just said," Charles insisted. "I just happened to walk over there with her."

"For tea, did you?"

"No. We were just talking. She had tea."

"You had tea, too," Tommie said in a quiet voice.

"I only ordered it to throw you some business, Ms. Watson. I didn't dare drink it," he countered.

"Why not?" she asked.

"Because I don't drink tea, and who knows what's in that stuff you concoct," he stated flatly.

Beverly Cantrell had been sitting in the office chair behind the desk, watching the interchange uneasily. Finbar turned the conversation to her.

"Is that true, Miss Cantrell? Charlie and Ms. Beadwell just happened to walk in together?" Finbar asked, turning his attention to Beverly.

"Well, yes, I suppose so. I came out before Charlie ... I mean, Charles did."

"I see. Did Charlie and Ms. Beadwell not come into the shop with you?"

"Oh, no, I came in before them. I got a couple of

cold drinks and brought them back to the gazebo. I had a lunch date with Henry, you know."

"Yeah. She just about broke her neck running out there when she saw him at the gazebo," Charles sneered. "Grabbed her lunch and took off like a bat outta hell. I couldn't imagine what the big hurry was, so I walked outside and saw Henry hunkered down behind a post. That's when Coral came over to harass me, and then we just walked on over to the tea shop with her flapping her yap nonstop."

"You should be careful running in them high heels, Miss Cantrell. You could break yer pretty legs," he said, making her giggle. "I've just met yer Henry Erving. He's a lovely man. Yer boyfriend, is that right? Seems like a good fellow," Holmes said.

"He is. He's a wonderful man."

"Been together long?"

"We … uh … no, not very long," she fumbled.

"Yes, he told me about how that Ms. Beadwell treated him. Led him on something shameful."

"She did. She was so mean. She didn't deserve his attention," she said, her face getting red again.

"No, she did not. It's good fortune the two of you found one another. I'm very happy for you."

"Thank you, Mr. Holmes. You're a nice man."

"You know, it makes me wonder if Coral was hateful to other people. Not just Henry. I heard she had a reputation as a bully. Did you like her, Beverly?"

Tommie asked. She seemed genuinely interested.

"Not really. I didn't dislike her, but I didn't like her either. She had a nasty temper, or so I was told, and she was very mean to Henry, throwing away his gifts and engineering that promotion like she did."

"I heard about that. Did you like her, Charles?"

"Take her or leave her. She was just the lady from the UPS Store next door. We didn't socialize," he said.

"She must not have been very good at her job."

"What makes you say that?" Charles asked.

"Well, one day I saw her yelling at you on the sidewalk. You were holding a package that looked like it was torn apart. She should've had better customer service than that, don't you think? It was her responsibility to report all damage to packages to the main office so they could deal with the negligent courier."

Instead of agreeing with her, Charles became angry. "Why don't you mind your own business, Ms. Watson? What were you doing, spying on me? I haven't done anything. It was just a package."

"No, I wasn't spying. I just noticed the two of you when I was cleaning tables in my shop. I don't think she should've been yelling at you like that." Tommie's face was the picture of innocence.

"For crying out loud, Charles. She wasn't attacking you. She was only sympathizing. Get off your high horse before you say something stupider," she barked. Then, remembering Holmes was in the room, she softened her tone. "Oh, we are all just so upset about Coral Beadwell. It's a wonder any of us can have civil conversations. I'm so sorry, everyone. I hope all this will resolve itself soon. Mr. Holmes, Ms. Watson. Thank you so much for coming in and letting us know we can release these other rentals to the public."

"Yes, and if there are any other Floribunda properties you'd be interesting in purchasing, Mr. Holmes, don't hesitate to call me. I'll be more than happy to take you on a tour around town to see them, and we can talk man to man," Charles said.

"I'll do that, Charlie," Finbar said.

"It's Charles," Charles said under his breath as he opened the door for them.

And with that, Tommie and Finbar were dismissed and left Floral Real Estate.

Chapter Fifteen

FIRST FLORIBUNDA BANK was just two blocks over from the real estate office, but it required driving in a complete square to reach it. Tommie took a right off the diagonal one-way Lantana Lane where they were parked and turned onto Oleander Street. Then, she took another right onto Coreopsis Road to Mimosa Street where the bank was located. Leaving the car in the parking lot between the First Floribunda Bank and the Historic Floral Bank, she and Finbar walked around on the sidewalk and entered the bank. When the Historic Floral Bank was turned into a museum, all the accounts and the contents of the safe deposit boxes were relocated into the new building. Architecturally, it lacked the beauty of the historic building and was basically a modern utilitarian structure. The only other bank in town was the Floral County Savings and Loan on Quince Street, so the locals split their business between the two.

Finbar and Tommie hoped Don Lareby and his

sisters would be available, and as luck would have it, they were. The three of them had cubicles in a shared office space with a window, and they were all at their desks without customers.

"Hi, Don. Hi, Susan. Hi, Elaine. I've popped in to introduce you to somebody who's just moved into town," Tommie said, giving them a dazzling smile.

Don stood and walked to his door opening. Susan and Elaine got up and propped their arms up on the low upholstered walls of their cubicles. Their motions were simultaneous and mirrored one another.

"This is Finbar Holmes. Mr. Holmes, this is Don Lareby," she said.

"How d'you do?" Finbar said, shaking Don's hand enthusiastically.

"Nice to meet you. I detect an accent," Don said.

"Right you are. I'm from Dublin, Ireland."

"Oh, Ireland! How exciting," Susan said.

"Finbar, this is Susan Clay," Tommie said, indicating the woman in the left cubicle.

Finbar shook the woman's extended hand.

"And this is Elaine Frank," Tommie said, indicating an identical woman in the right cubicle.

"So pleased to meet you both. Such beautiful lassies. Might you be sisters?" Finbar asked.

Susan gigged, and Elaine emitted a similar sound.

"How could you tell?" Elaine asked.

"Oh, but 'tis like I'm surrounded by lovely spring

flowers," he replied, a flirtatious air to his voice as he thickened his accent.

Both women seemed to swoon. Tommie noticed they were wearing similar dresses with floral prints. She resisted the urge to roll her eyes.

"What brings you to Floribunda, Mr. Holmes?" Don asked, ignoring his sisters' antics.

"I wanted a warm climate to bask in the sun, and the name caught me eye and 'twas musical on me tongue. So here I am in the midst of all this flowery magic," Finbar said, his voice lilting.

"I'm so happy you're here. Maybe you can tell us all about Ireland," Susan said.

"Yes, we'd very much like to visit there someday," Elaine chimed in.

"Ah, 'twould be me pleasure. Perhaps over a suppa tea at Ms. Watson's establishment," he said.

Their faces drooped, and so did Don's, at the mention of the tea shop. It was clear the event had upset them terribly. They avoided looking at her and hemmed and hawed nervously.

"I understand how you feel. I don't know if I'll ever get over the fact that somebody we know died in my shop," Tommie said.

"Oh, now Tommie. It wasn't your fault. We know that, for cripes sake. As much as we've gone in and had tea, we've always felt your place was so clean," Susan said. "I don't care what Charles Williams says."

"Me neither. Linda Beadwell was in here yesterday, and she tried to say your tea blend was bad, but I told her she didn't know what she was talking about. She doesn't even drink tea, for cripes sake," Elaine stated.

"Yes, 'tis true. Ms. Watson made me a sup of tea last night, and I slept like a bare-bummed babe. She's a wonder with them herbs. I'd trust her wit' me life, I would," Finbar said, "but I'm wondering, what d'you think happened to the poor woman?"

"Well, let me tell you. We were sitting two tables over. Coral was sitting alone in her usual spot with her usual teacup. She was predictable, you know what I mean? Even her sack lunch was the same as always. Ham and cheese sandwich on white bread, a single-serve bag of barbecue potato chips, fat dill pickle, and three oatmeal cookies," Don said.

"Not two, not four, but three," Susan and Elaine said in unison with a guilty laugh.

"Always the same," Don said with a shrug.

"Curious woman, it seems," Finbar remarked.

"Yes. She banked here, you know," Don said. "She lived in the historic Beadwell House on Bottlebrush Boulevard. It's number seven on the historic trail—a colonial two-story home with columns and a balcony. It used to be a larger mansion, but they took out the walkways between the main house and the wings. Tom— that's her brother—and Linda Beadwell live in the West Wing. They converted it into a stand-alone house and cut in a new front door facing King's Mantle Street. We secured their building loan. The East Wing was sold to the Blakes, and they turned it into Blake's Bed 'n' Breakfast. People call it the 'B B 'n' B' because Blake's Bed 'n' Breakfast is too much of a tongue-twister. We secured their renovation loan, too. Coral had lived in the main house by herself the past four years since her folks died."

"I hear Linda wants that historic house real bad," Susan said.

"She's cheesed because Tom didn't get it in the parents' will," Elaine said. "I guess she'll get it now."

"Not necessarily, Sisters. The terms of the will stated Tom would have right of first refusal to *buy* the house, just like Coral did. She *bought* the house, and the money went to some charity her parents had designated," Don said.

"How did you know that, Donny?" Susan asked.

"I heard it from Petey Smith at the poker game last night. Petey's the Beadwell's attorney. A few of us guys get together and play cards once a week. You're welcome to join us, Mr. Holmes."

"I may well do that, Mr. Lareby. I like the cards almost as much as the horses," Finbar said with a wink.

"Great. Call me Don."

"If you'll call me Finbar."

"It's a deal."

"Who's handling the sale of Coral's house now that she's deceased?" Tommie asked.

"Floral Real Estate, who else?" Elaine said.

"So, Charles Williams gets to put more money in his pockets," Tommie said with a sigh.

"Well, the way I hear it, he has to split it with Beverly Cantrell ... again! They got equal commissions on the first sale, and they'll get the same if Tom and Linda buy it." Susan joined her sister in a conspiratorial nod.

"No! I can't believe Charles would do that," Tommie said, her eyes wide.

"I don't think he wants to, but it's stipulated in the will. The parents died on the same night, believe it or not. Car accident. Charles and Beverly had a knock-down-drag-out shouting match outside our window four years ago when the will was read. We all heard the fight. And then yesterday, when Linda Beadwell was in here, she was complaining about Beverly getting half the commission again," Don said.

"That's right, she didn't complain about Charles, though," Susan said.

"No, not about Charles," Elaine confirmed.

"Just Beverly," they said in unison.

"Wow. I guess Henry Erving will be glad when the house sells and Beverly Cantrell gets that big commission," Tommie commented.

The three of them looked at her blankly.

"What? Why are you looking at me like that?"

"Why on earth would Henry Erving benefit from Beverly's commission, for cripes sake?" Susan asked.

"Aren't they a thing?" Tommie asked.

"What? No. He had a thing for Coral Beadwell. I thought everybody knew that," Elaine said. "He was truly lovesick."

"Now he's just sick," Susan quipped.

"Tommie's new, Sisters. She can't know everything," Don said.

"But I thought Henry and Beverly were dating. They were eating together in the gazebo Monday," Tommie stated.

"I saw that, too, but it wasn't Henry's doing, them having lunch in that gazebo," Susan said.

"Nope. We were walking over for lunch. Henry was in the gazebo. I saw Beverly come running out the door of the real estate office, cross the street, go in your shop, and come running back to the gazebo. On those high heels, if you can imagine. It's a wonder she didn't break her neck, for cripes sake," Elaine said.

"Henry plays poker with us. He's never mentioned Beverly, but he talked a lot … and I mean *a lot* … about Coral. He was obsessed with her, and she was hateful as could be to him," Don confirmed. "Once, he said she made him so mad he wanted to throttle her. He wouldn't, though. Henry's a pretty harmless, mild-mannered kind of guy."

Susan and Elaine exchanged a look, and then gave Tommie the same look. *Not so harmless, huh?* she thought.

Don Lareby glanced at his watch. "Hey, it's almost lunchtime. We're walking down the street to The Lunch Pad. It's a space exploration themed diner just past your tea shop, Tommie. They have a good *Full Moon Pie* dessert. Y'all want to come along and eat with us?"

"Alas. 'Twould be lovely, I'm sure, but Ms. Watson has been on her broken ankle far too long today, so I'll be taking her back to her house. But, sure, one day soon we'll go," Finbar said.

"That's great, and you'll think about the poker club, too, right?" Don said, shaking his hand.

"Sure. Sure. 'Twill be on me list," Finbar replied.

"And Tommie, don't you worry. As soon as your shop is back open, we'll be there," Susan said.

"Yes, Tommie, we love you. Take care of that ankle, and thanks for bringing Finbar to meet us. We're thrilled, just thrilled to have him here," Elaine said.

"Bye, now," the three of them said in unison.

Finbar helped Tommie into the car, and they drove back home for lunch.

Chapter Sixteen

LUNCH AT FINBAR'S was leftover breakfast. In Tommie's estimation, it was just as good the second time around. She ate heartily, helped Finbar clear the dishes, and took up her spot on the sofa.

Finbar sat in his armchair, lifted his feet onto the ottoman, and took his legal pad in hand. The three dogs (he said Sherlock had requested the presence of Zed and Red) laid on the floor and finished licking their chops after receiving the last bits of black pudding and bacon.

"I would say we had a productive morning, d'you agree?" Finbar asked.

"Definitely. Let's get it on paper before we forget the details," Tommie suggested.

"Righto. I'm listing our suspects as we interviewed them. This is my notepad setup." He took a second legal pad from the end table and showed her. At the top of the first page was written: SUSPECT INTERVIEWS. Below that was written: SUSPECT 1:

He filled in the name SARAH BETH BREWSTER beside it. Underneath her name were listed topics with several lines between each:

> INTERVIEWED AT:
> MOTIVE:
> ALIBI:
> LIES:
> TRUTHS:

On the second page, the topics were:

> IMPLICATES:
> GOSSIP & HEARSAY:
> QUESTIONS:
> OBSERVATIONS:

The following page began a new chart with SUSPECT 2: Beside it, Finbar wrote: HENRY ERVING. He filled in the rest of the suspect names on the subsequent pages.

"That's amazing. You are the most organized man I've ever met," she said.

"Elementary, my dear Watson. It's just a technique to help me get my thoughts in order. It's easier for me to see it to get it in my brain. Right then. Sarah Beth Brewster. Interviewed at Brewster's Coffee Shoppe. Motive we leave blank and fill it in after some discussion.

Ah. Now, this one is very important. Alibi. Where was Mrs. Brewster at the time of the murder?"

"She said she wanted to get groceries at *Winn Dixie,* so she closed up early. She sent Linda Beadwell out the back door."

"Precisely. Now, do you recall if we caught her in any lies? Anything that you would consider untrue?"

Tommie thought for a few minutes. "No. Not at the moment. She said she was late opening up, but we can't verify that until we interview Linda Beadwell. I know they were arguing just before I opened at 12:00, and she confirmed it. I heard Sarah Beth's door slam shut just before mine opened. No, Finbar, I can't find any lies."

"What can we verify as true, then? She closed up her shop before 12:00. Mrs. Beadwell was in her shop until that time. Right?"

"Yes. Pretty much. Oh, and she saw Charles Williams outside walking with Coral. That's another reason she hurried Linda out of the shop, so she wouldn't have to deal with Charles. Where do we put all that about the affair?"

"That goes on the line labeled GOSSIP & HEARSAY. We'll come to that later."

"Cool. Works for me," she said, adjusting her position on the sofa.

"Who would you say she may have implicated in her testimony?"

"I'd say mostly Charles Williams, but maybe

Linda Beadwell, too."

"I agree. Now for Gossip. Charles and Linda's affair. Questions. I should like to know more about that argument and why she was tardy in the morning. Observations? None right now, so we leave it blank. Right, then. I think we're done with her for now."

He passed the legal pad to her for closer inspection, and Tommie was able to see at a glance the particulars they discussed surrounding the first suspect.

SUSPECT 1: SARAH BETH BREWSTER

INTERVIEWED AT: Brewster's Coffee Shoppe

MOTIVE:

ALIBI: Closed early for groceries & to avoid Charles Williams

LIES: Must verify reasons for tardiness & early closure

TRUTHS: Closed early; sent Linda Beadwell out back

IMPLICATES: Charles Williams, Linda Beadwell

GOSSIP & HEARSAY: Charles & Linda affair

QUESTIONS: details of argument; why late opening?

OBSERVATIONS:

"That looks great, Finbar. It puts everything in a perspective that's quick and easy to check off. I like it," she said, handing him back the legal pad.

"Lovely. Next is Henry Erving. Let's discuss Suspect Two."

"Let me try this one, Finbar, since you did the interview with Henry."

"Brilliant. I am quite delighted you are so engaged in our investigation. Proceed."

"OK. Interviewed at UPS Store. Motive unknown. No, wait. I think he has motives. He was passed over for promotion because of Coral. Also, she publicly made fun of him and spurned him. Those are pretty strong motives, don't you think?"

"Loss of income. Humiliation. Jealousy. Unrequited love. Those are very strong motives indeed. Good on you, Thomasina."

Tommie smiled and sat up straighter. "Alibi. He was in the gazebo having lunch with Beverly. I saw them myself. Lie? I don't know, unless what he said about Beverly being his girlfriend is untrue like the sisters said. You know, I really think I would have heard about it if they were an item ... unless it was a brand-new relationship that day. How about put 'relationships with Coral and Beverly' under questions?"

"Good thinking. For truth, we will say he watched Coral and Charles go in together. His testimony implicates Charles Williams, I think."

"And himself. I think he implicated himself, too. And the gossip is that Charles and Coral were an item. Henry put that out there to throw us off, I believe.

Questions? Like I said, his relationship with Coral Beadwell is a big question, and so is his relationship with Beverly."

"Right you are. Here, missus. You write out the next one whilst I put us on a fresh kettle of tea. I have a throat," he said, handing her the pad.

"What's that mean? You have a throat?" she asked.

"My throat is dry. I'm thirsty," he replied, hanging his tongue out his mouth.

Tommie chuckled. *What an odd turn of phrase for an odd sort of man,* she thought. *But I do like him very much.*

"Suspect Three is Beverly Cantrell. Interviewed at Floral Real Estate. Motive is jealousy over Henry. Alibi? She had a lunch date with Henry in the gazebo. Lie? It seems there was no set date and she simply went where she knew he was. Truth? She was in the gazebo with Henry when Coral died. And she saw Charles and Coral walk to the shop and go in together, which implicates Charles again. Gossip? I don't recall any except the sisters said Beverly did *not* have a thing with Henry. Questions? I want to know how long she and Henry have been together."

"I do, as well. D'you remember what Charlie said about her running outside when she saw Henry. Peculiar behavior to run across the street in those high heels like that. And there was some other gossip about Beverly, was there not, from the sisters and brother?"

"You're right! Let me think. They said Beverly and Charles split the commission on the sale of Beadwell House to Coral. And she fought with Charles about it four years ago. That's motive—a big commission if Coral is out of the way and her brother buys the historic home. Oh! Oh! And they said Henry Erving was hopelessly smitten with Coral. We'll have to put that under Henry as a lie."

"No, missus. Put it under gossip until we confirm it."

"Oh, I get it. A lie is only a lie if we can prove it. Same thing with the truth. Just like in a courtroom, huh?"

"Precisely. We must deal in facts and either prove or disprove any innuendos or our speculations," Holmes said, returning to the living room with the teapot.

Finbar poured a steaming mug of tea for both of them and brought Tommie the honey blend and a spoon. He laid an object on the end table beside him, and Tommie could see it was a pipe with a large bowl and an arched stem. She waited for him to explain, but he didn't.

"You be the scribe now whilst we complete suspect number four, missus," he said.

"OK. Suspect four is Charles Williams. Interviewed at Floral Real Estate. He has plenty of motive to kill Coral *and* to implicate me: he didn't like her—I'm pretty sure she opened at least one of his packages. And he wants my shop."

"That's revenge and greed, for sure. What's his motive for killing Ms. Beadwell?"

"Could it be revenge for her treatment of him and for tampering with his deliveries?"

"Possibly, but there must be more than just ill feelings to be a motive."

"You're right. That's a good question, though. His motive would be more focused on me. By having a death in my shop, it discredits me and my business practices," she said.

"That's a very good point, Thomasina. We've not considered the ripple effect of having the death occur in yer establishment and to pin the blame on you. We must think of that in terms of motive for some of our other suspects. Off hand, I wonder if we should list that as a motive for Mrs. Brewster? Would she benefit from you going out of business?'

"Wow. Didn't think of that. She would certainly say it didn't, but I do remember her being very upset when Coral convinced the LCO—the Ladies' Charity Organization—to hold their monthly meetings in Watson's. It's a good deal of business because it generated repeat customers throughout the week. That would give her a motive for both me and Coral." She flipped back to the first page and amended her entry for Sarah Beth, adding revenge and loss of business as motives. "Dangit, Finbar. This opens up a whole can of worms if I'm thrown into the mix as a target!"

"It does, missus, but we must consider it. Would Beverly profit as well from you losing yer shop clientele?"

"Not anymore. If I had lost my shop, I would've had to move into a less expensive house. But, because I'm renting from you now instead of her, that won't be the case. On the flip side, she can't collect any cleaning or move out fees or any more dog deposits, and she has to return my initial deposit," she said.

"Ah, but you forget. The murder occurred *before* we made *our* agreement. As far as she knew, she would be able to extort yer situation because you would have to find a new residence. So, Thomasina, we must list that as a motive for Beverly. D'you see how the spiderweb begins to enlarge?"

"You're not kidding," she said, blowing out a breath of air. "Let's finish with Charles. Alibi. He was watching Henry in the gazebo, then he walked to the shop and came in with Coral."

"Neither of those is an alibi. It places him directly at the scene. Yer flustered now and not thinking straight. His only chance at an alibi is that he was sitting away from Coral when she died. But, there again, that doesn't account for him being in proximity to her cup at the time she took it from you." He looked at her with interest, waiting for her deduction.

"Charles doesn't really have an alibi," she stated.

"No, lad. He does not." He upturned his mug and drank the last of his tea. Then, he leaned back against the chair, took the pipe, and hung the stem onto the corner of his mouth.

"That's a classic Sherlock Holmes kind of pipe. Do you actually smoke that?" she asked.

"This? Oh, no, dear girl. This is a replica of the cherrywood pipe from the Sir Arthur Conan Doyle stories. Mine is crafted from African Mahogany wood and has a Meerschaum insert bowl. It's sometimes called a calabash pipe, although it is not made from a melon. I used to smoke fags."

"Probably shouldn't say that here in America," she warned. "It'll be misconstrued."

"Hm. Perhaps not. Cigarettes, then. I gave up the habit. The pipe here gives me the feel of having one in my mouth without actually smoking. I feel it helps me concentrate," he explained.

"Now you really look like the legendary detective," she said with an amused smile.

"Quite. Continue please, missus," he said with a slight dismissive wave of his hand.

"OK. Charles lied when he said he drank coffee and not tea, because he ordered tea … exactly the same drink as Coral."

"But he did not drink his tea. He only bought it."

"True. That could be because he either didn't like drinking tea or he thought the blend was bad. That's speculation again. Truth? He walked over with Coral, and they entered together. That's all I can say. Oh! And he touched her teacup."

"Did he, now?" He shifted the pipe to the other side of his mouth and learned forward.

"Yes. He grabbed her cup. She got mad, and I gave him the second cup. Come to think of it, Beverly touched the teacups, as well. Yikes."

"That goes under yer observations, Thomasina. Let's finish up with his interview, and then you can go back and write down yer observation on Beverly's list. Whom does Charlie implicate?"

"No one ... except me."

"Right. He does at that. Gossip is the same as that for Beverly. They had to split the sales moneys."

"Questions. Oh, I have so many, but I don't know how to even start. I'm a little confused right now," she admitted with chagrin.

"Have a sup of your tea. Then, I want to hear why *you* suspect each of them," Holmes said.

Tommie finished up her tea while Holmes sucked on his empty pipe. When she had drained her cup, she wiped the fine bead of sweat beneath her nose.

"Sarah Beth Brewster. She has means but not much motive. She was not in the shop, but she *does* have a key and can come in any time she wants. She wouldn't want to put me out of business, even though I have the Episcopal women. That's only 28 people. And as far as holding a grudge for Coral's involvement with giving me that business, I don't see it as so significant. If I went out of business, Sarah Beth couldn't pick up the lease on my place, and Charles Williams couldn't buy it. It belongs to my cousin Sanderson Harper. It's a family holding and can't be sold without a family member's name on the deed. Harper is my maiden name. Sarah Beth even offered to front me money to relocate in case you wouldn't let me stay here," she said.

"That's very kind of her. Henry Erving?"

"I think he has pretty good motive, but I don't know if he has the means. How could he have tainted the teacup? He came in *after* Coral died. I suppose he could've had an accomplice, but that's unlikely. He told a lot of half truths about Coral and Beverly. That bears more questioning. If he'll meet you for a drink, you can probably get more information. If he's all right, that is. He mopped up the poisoned tea with napkins, and it was all over his hands."

"Yes, he seemed rather ill when we talked to him. Fits the symptoms of cyanide exposure. We should check on him again this afternoon, d'you think?"

"Wouldn't be a bad idea, just to be sure. Do you think he could have purposely cleaned up to get just enough on his hands to get sick? To throw attention away from him?"

"It's a possibility we should consider. Continue."

"Beverly Cantrell touched the teacups. I had forgotten all about it. She ran in and got a couple of drinks from the coolers, and when she put her money on the counter, she bumped her hand against the teacups in the caddies."

"Is that where Ms. Beadwell's cup was?" he asked.

"Not in the caddies, but just beside them. I kept it separated because it's the only one she likes ... liked ... to drink from. Beverly could easily have dropped poison into the cup or smeared it on the rim."

"And Charlie? You said he touched Coral's cup directly," Holmes said.

"He did. He grabbed it and pulled it toward himself. She got ticked off and told him to let it go. They argued about it. I was so focused on their faces I didn't even look at their hands. He could have been putting poison in her cup while she and I were distracted by the argument they were having."

"A distinct possibility."

"Wait, Finbar, we didn't profile Don and his sisters yet."

"No, and we shan't. After interviewing them, I am convinced they do not qualify as suspects. They were, as you said, extras on a film set. They are most important, though. They seem to have a direct line with the local gossip, so I believe it is in our best interest to cultivate them as sources ... like confidential informants. What d'you think?"

"I couldn't agree with you more. We have one real suspect left to interview, and I happen to know exactly where she will be at 4:00 this afternoon—St.

Mary's Catholic Church. You said you like betting on horses, Finbar, and playing card games. How about we go play some Bingo?" she said with a grin.

Chapter Seventeen

ST. MARY'S CATHOLIC CHURCH ran the best Bingo game in town. In fact, it ran the only Bingo game in town. Because it was held in the church, and the proceeds went to charity, people tended not to consider it gambling. The fact that money was spent to buy the cards and it was a game of chance did not matter to the locals. The church sanctioned it, and Father Horace Duncan was the number caller. It was a booming business for those who did not have Wednesday evening services, so there were few, if any, Protestants in attendance at the games.

Tommie and Finbar bought game cards when they entered the door of the large Bingo room. Looking around the rows of tables, Tommie spotted Linda Beadwell at the third one on the right in the second row. There were two empty seats beside her. She pointed them out to Finbar and sent him over to commandeer them before someone else did, she having to hop along more slowly. He slipped through the meandering players and grabbed both chairs beside Linda, just as a large woman in an oversized t-shirt and yoga pants was about to claim one of them.

"Sorry, madam," he said, "but I'm holding this for my friend. She is handicapped. Thank you, kindly."

The woman looked as though she would fight for the chair, but when she saw Tommie limping over, she shrugged and went to another table. Finbar settled Tommie in one chair, and he sat in the one nearest Linda.

"So, tell me now, lad. How is this Bingo game played?" he asked.

"It's pretty simple. Your card is a grid of 25 numbers below five letters that spell B, I, N, G, O. The Priest calls out a letter and a number. You look on your card. If you have it, you cover it with a colored token. When you get a full line covered either horizontally, vertically, or diagonally, you call out 'Bingo!' for the win," Tommie explained.

"Ah, 'tis simple, indeed," he said, laying on the accent for the benefit of Linda beside him. "It sounds grand." He turned to Linda, who was carefully arranging her Bingo paraphernalia on the table, which included several small knick-knacks—a stuffed kitten, a black obsidian rock, a tiny jar of pink salt, and a naked resin troll with garish fuzzy green hair.

Finbar pointed to the figurine. "I do like yer be-baws, lass. That one in particular. He looks to be a leprechaun much like meself?"

Linda gave him a startled look, reflexively smoothing the green hair of the doll. "It's a troll," she muttered under her breath.

"Ah, is it, indeed? How like a leprechaun he is. I hope himself brings you some Irish luck." He laughed, and she almost did. "But lass, I see you have no tokens for yer cards. What d'you do when you get a number?

Linda gave him a closer look. He was a comical sight, with his wispy hair, large ears, and blinking sky-blue eyes, and she caught herself before she laughed at him.

"I have my daubers," she replied, indicating the fat cylindrical self-inking fluorescent stamps on the table.

"Ah, 'tis a clever woman, you are. And I see you have cards a-plenty. D'you not use them over? But, sure, you cannot if you daub them, eh?"

"No, I buy sets of disposable paper cards. They're four to a page, so I can play four cards at once."

"Oh, that's lovely. Ms. Watson, why did we not get the multiple chances to win like ... I'm sorry, lass. We've not been introduced. I'm Finbar Holmes, formerly from Dublin, but now from Floribunda," he said with a flourish, extending his hand.

Linda took it reluctantly and shook it. "I'm Mrs. Linda Beadwell. My family was born and raised here in Floral County," she said with a sniff. She leaned forward and regarded Tommie coolly. "Hello, Ms. Watson. Are you two together?"

Before Tommie could answer her, Holmes

continued talking. "Oh yes. Missus Watson is my tenant, meself now the owner of a duplex house on Camelia Street. D'you know Camelia Street? 'Tis a right pretty little place. Where might you be living, Missus Beadwell?"

"I know where you're talking about,' she said with another exaggerated sniff. "I live in the large historic colonial house on the corner of King's Mantle Street and Bottlebrush Boulevard."

"Oh, is that the grand house with the flag flying in front?" he asked.

"No, that's the main house, the historic Beadwell House. Mine is the West Wing House. They were formerly joined by a covered walkway. But I'll soon be rejoining the houses with a new walkway and moving into the main house."

"Now that's a right smart move, lass. 'Twill be ever so much nicer to have a grand mansion to call yer own. Good on you. I've got a thirst. Have they something to drink here?"

"They have coffee and tea on that back table, but you'd better hurry. Father Duncan will be pulling numbers soon," she said.

Finbar got up and headed for the refreshment table, leaving Tommie to interview Linda.

"Linda, I'm so sorry about your sister-in-law. I'm sure Tom is very upset. Is there anything I can do for you?" she said, showing sincere sympathy.

"I think you've done quite enough, don't you?"

Linda quipped, giving Tommie an icy look.

"Linda, I had nothing to do with Coral's death. It just happened to be in my shop."

"I think, if you had better sanitary procedures, it would not have occurred at all," she accused.

"That's not true. Coral's death was foul play, Linda. It was no accident and had nothing to do with hygiene or sanitary procedures. Someone else caused it."

"That's crap, and you know it. I saw your cups just sitting out there exposed on your counter. Anything could get on them. And those canisters where anybody could just open them and contaminate their contents. And your so-called natural remedies. You're not a doctor. You don't have any kind of license to dispense medicines, but you put a bunch of herbs and ingredients together and call them medicines. Thomas is a pharmacist, and he told me it was just a matter of time before somebody died from one of your supposed cures. You're a menace, Tommie Watson, and we're glad you're closed down," she hissed, her tone of voice full of malice.

"Really, Linda? And just what were you doing in my shop that day Coral died? You don't drink tea, so why did you sneak in my back door?"

"That's a lie! Who says I was in your shop?" Linda said, her voice a trifle too loud.

"I heard you come in, and I saw you leave out the back door," Tommie said, eyes narrowed.

Linda sat with her mouth open, and then she

shook her Prince Valiant hair back from her face and stared fixedly at her cards.

"So, Linda. Why were you in my shop before I opened for business?" Tommie pressed.

"I had to use the bathroom. Is that a crime?"

"It's not a crime, but it's odd, considering you just live three blocks away."

"I . . . it was an emergency."

"Sarah Beth has a bathroom. Why didn't you use hers in the coffee shop?"

"Because she forced me out, and I didn't want him to see me," she barked.

"Him?"

"You're twisting my words. She forced me out, and I didn't want anyone to see me. I couldn't wait to go all the way home. That's what I mean. You stop harassing me, Ms. Watson. You caused my sister-in-law's death. That's all I know. Now leave me alone!" She shouted.

People all around the Bingo hall twisted in their seats to get a look at the commotion as Linda Beadwell huffily gathered up her cards, daubers, and good luck idols, and moved them to another table. Tommie sat still, red-faced with embarrassment. Finbar approached and casually sat down, benignly sipping from a Styrofoam cup of tea until the room settled down.

"That went well, missus," he remarked.

"Yeah, just great. I've probably lost a dozen more customers in that short exchange, but I think I got some useful information," she said with a half-smile.

"Did you, now? Good work. Shall we go?"

"Don't you want to stay and play our cards?"

"Nah, never was so thrilled with the Bingo. Moves too slow for me," he said, helping her stand.

"Wait. What? You've played Bingo before?"

"Of course, I have, Watson. Am I not Catholic?"

Chapter Eighteen

OFFICER EARL PETRY called that night after Tommie got home from Finbar's home, and she was in a great mood. Together, she and Holmes had finished filling out Linda's interview chart, being sure to note her argumentative demeaner and the blatant lies they had uncovered. Other relevant observations and deliberate misrepresentations they noted included her reference to not only moving into the main house but joining her current house to it to make it even larger. Tommie pointed out Linda's slip of the tongue excuse about not wanting "him" to see her. Tommie was certain that meant Charles Williams. She felt Linda had strong motives, and Finbar agreed.

Tommie had already fed the dogs and was nibbling on a grilled cheese sandwich when Earl called.

"Hello, Ms. Tommie Watson. This is Officer Earl Petry. How are you holding up tonight?" he asked.

His bass voice was smooth and melodious, and it made her stomach flutter.

"Pretty good, Earl. What's going on with you?" she asked, glad that he called. Though Tommie was not on the dating market at the moment, she found Earl Petry more than attractive, with his smoldering smokey eyes, heavy brows, close cut silver hair, and neatly trimmed white beard. (Tommie was a sucker for facial hair.) Should she decide to put herself out there again, Earl would be at the top of her list.

"I wanted to let you know that you're no longer an official suspect. You are now just a person of interest."

"I like that. A 'person of interest' sounds a whole lot better, anyway."

He laughed, and she found herself smiling broadly, though he couldn't see her through the phone.

"That doesn't mean you're off the hook, Tommie, and your shop is still closed because it's a crime scene. I'm sorry about that."

"Yeah, I know." She sighed. It had been an exhausting day. "When do you suppose I can get in there to clean up?"

"A day or two, but don't go in there anymore."

"What makes you say that? Did someone tell you I had been in there?" She kept her tone guarded.

"Oh, come on, Tommie. Number one, you're an independent woman who does what she pleases. Number two, you're a woman whose shop is very important to her current lifestyle. And number three, I could see where you dragged your boot in the fingerprint dust."

"Oh," she said quietly, her face reddening.

"Darlin', I know you want to be in there to get your herbs and things sorted out, but I have to ask you to keep your distance for a few more days until I say it's cleared. Please?"

"All right, Earl. But only because you asked me. Can you tell me if you've found out anything about how Coral died?" she asked.

"Um hmm. She was poisoned, but you already knew that. It was likely cyanide … just like Sandy told you," he said.

"But … I … um."

"Lord, Tommie. I like you a lot, and that's why I'm going to trust you with information you really shouldn't have just yet. I'm not a stupid man, and you're not a stupid woman, so it's best if we're honest with each other. OK?"

"OK, Earl. I'm sorry." She was genuinely embarrassed and felt like an adolescent middle-school girl with a crush.

"No need. But, let's don't try to herd cats. I'll tell you whatever I can, and you leave it at that. Coral Beadwell was murdered. She was poisoned, and it appears to be cyanide. It didn't come from any of your product. It was placed in her cup before you fixed her tea. There was a significant amount, and she didn't have a chance of survival, so Sandy says. What I want to know is, do you have any idea how it got there, Tommie?"

"Earl, I don't. I promise you. I'm extremely fastidious about sanitizing those teacups and all my equipment. The cups are always washed each night, even the ones that haven't been used. When they're dry, I stack them in the caddies, covered with a clean linen tea towel, just before I lock up to go home. The only way they could be tainted is for someone to put that poison in or on them before I open the door at 12:00, or for somebody to do it unnoticed while I'm serving customers or preparing their tea."

"You told me Linda Beadwell was in your shop before you opened up at noon."

"Yes, she was, Earl. She even admitted it."

"How did you not see her when she came in?"

"I was on my hands and knees in the *Alice in Wonderland* window display—the 'Mad Hatter Tea-Party' one to the left of the front door."

"I saw it. Very novel."

Tommie was silent, not knowing if he meant the display was novel or if he was being clever and trying to make a joke of it being about a book. When he didn't say anything more, she continued talking about Linda.

"I heard the back door open, and I tried to look, but I couldn't see anyone over the bookcases. After I scooted out and turned my sign, I happened to notice Linda leaving out the back door. She said she had an emergency and had to use my bathroom, then she said she was in there hiding from a man."

"She told you all this on Monday?"

"No. Tonight at the Catholic Church, at Bingo."

"I didn't know you played Bingo, Tommie. Are you Catholic?"

"I'm not Catholic, and no, I don't play Bingo. I took Mr. Holmes there to inves ... uh ... to in*vite* him for Bingo."

"Good save, Tommie, but not good enough. You took him there to investigate Linda Beadwell. Isn't that what you meant to say?"

"No, no," she said with a nervous chuckle. "I was only trying to find him something to do, and surprise, surprise. Linda was there, too. We got to talking and she might have let a few things slip."

"And you might have helped her along. Lord, Tommie. You are something else."

"I wanted to know why she was in my shop before I opened and why she was sneaking around. That's all I was doing."

"OK, OK. Do you know if she could have come to the counter by the cups and you didn't see her?"

"Sure. I was facing the opposite direction (*with my big butt up in the air*, she didn't say), and I don't know if you're aware, but I'm a little bit height challenged, especially in that position on my hands and knees. If Linda was quiet, I would never have known she was there.

I only saw her leave because I turned around from unlocking the door."

"Any other people around those cups on your counter at any time?"

"Yes, as a matter of fact. Beverly Cantrell bumped against them when she put her money beside the cash register at 12:05, and then Charles Williams actually put his hands around Coral's cup at 12:20. I told you that, already."

"What about Don Lareby and his sisters?"

"No. They came in after I had already served Coral. They were nowhere near."

"How about Henry?"

"He came in afterwards, too. Oh my gosh! I meant to check on Henry tonight. He mopped up the tea, and I'm sure he got poison on his hands. I saw him this morning, and he seemed really ill."

"He's doing all right. They checked him out at Floribunda Urgent Care this afternoon. He was a pretty sick guy."

"Cyanide poisoning?" Her voice was a whisper.

"Yes. Transdermal poisoning. It was a good thing Henry went and got himself checked out. The poison had been in his system since Monday. Apparently, your Irish landlord Mr. Holmes called and suggested he go," Earl confirmed.

"My gosh. That's a relief," she said.

"Sandy told me you were spared because you

used that plastic bag from your pocket to touch the cup and wet napkins. Still, it scared the crap out of me. You've got to be more careful, Darlin'. Sometimes the nicest towns have the worst people living in them."

"I will, Earl. I promise. What happens now?"

"We'll continue our investigation. I have to insist that you work from home, if you can. If you need, I can bring over your unopened herbs from the storeroom for you. We didn't bother them," he offered.

"I have plenty here in my office. Can I make up anything special for you?" she asked hopefully.

"Yeah. How about fix me a *Keep-Tommie-Watson-out-of-Trouble* potion?"

"Sorry, that's a recipe I don't know how to follow very well."

"I don't doubt that. Stay out of your shop, Tommie, until I tell you it's all clear. Can you do that for me, please?"

"For you, I absolutely will," she said with a smile.

Chapter Nineteen

THURSDAY, VALENTINE'S DAY, would have been a lucrative day for Watson's, but because her shop would not be open, Tommie decided to give her friend Sarah Beth a gift. After Earl's phone call, she was no longer tired. The conversation and his sexy voice had inspired her to create some treats that would pair well with coffee. She called Sarah Beth and asked to meet her at Brewster's in the morning at 5:45. Then, she began prepping.

She first assembled the makings for *Besame Bagel Bites. Besame* was Spanish for "kiss me." Taking the bite-sized premade bagels from the freezer, she laid them on the counter to thaw while she mixed up a sweet syrup of milk, sugar, butter, and poppyseeds. She warmed it over a low heat until it was liquified and set the syrup aside to cool in a lidded glass bowl. In the morning, she would toast the bagels before going to Brewster's and heat the syrup in Sarah Beth's microwave for drizzling over the crispy chewy pastries.

Next, she made her *Salty Sweetheart Mix* by combining pumpkin seeds, quartered fig filled cookies, dried cranberries, pretzel bits, butter mints, and dark chocolate pieces. After tossing the mixture to distribute the sweet and salty ingredients, she portioned out ¼ cup servings in zipper lock snack bags. Sarah Beth could put them on the tables for the customers to sample while they drank their morning brews.

Finally, she finished up the *Double Sweet Kisses* she had planned to serve at her own shop. She melted milk chocolate in a double boiler until it was creamy. Then, she took Hershey's Kisses candies which had been covered in creamy peanut butter and frozen on baking sheets and set them flat side down on crisscrossed cooling racks. She carefully spooned melted chocolate over them, letting the excess chocolate pool on the baking sheets beneath the candies. She placed the racks and sheets into the refrigerator to harden and set her clock to get up early. She sent Finbar a text telling him she'd be gone in the morning, and then she showered and went to bed.

When the cuckoo clock on her cell phone sounded the alarm at 5:00, Tommie stumbled around like a boozer with a hangover. She splashed her face with water and brushed her short hair. Putting on a clean pair of red scrubs for the occasion, she depressed the switch on her electric kettle to boil some water for tea. Then, she put the candies in a Rubbermaid canister and placed them in a soft sided cooler, along with the container of syrup and the bagged sweet and salty mix. She prepared herself a cup of Red Rooibos tea with honey and sipped it while she watched the bagels brown up in her countertop convection oven. She wrapped the toasted bagels in a dishtowel and put them in a cloth tote, told the dogs to be good, and headed outside to her car.

Sarah Beth was waiting for her at 5:45 in the back of the store. They carried the treats inside and sorted them. Tommie heated the syrup in the microwave and carefully drizzled it over the bagel bites, while Sarah Beth stacked the sweet and salty mix bags on the back counter beside the trays of *Besame Bagel Bites* and *Double Sweet Kisses* and placed Tommie's labeled notecards beside each treat.

"I can't believe you're doing this for me. These should've been for *your* customers," she lamented, casting a glance over her shoulder at Tommie.

"Well, if I can't use them, why shouldn't you? Besides, it makes me feel like I'm working in my own shop, somehow. Are you going to sell them or give them away for free?"

"I'm selling them, of course!" she exclaimed, holding up a card with a price marked on it.

"Look. There's Charles Williams coming across the street. Oh! There's Linda Beadwell's car at the curb. Maybe I should slip out back," Tommie said.

"Oh, no, you will not. You can help me behind the counter, if that's OK," Sarah Beth said as she turned her sign and unlocked her door. "Large drinks, $7.50; small drinks five bucks. Snacks are listed on the cards beside them. Here we go."

Tommie was glad to oblige and, judging from the steady influx of customers at just after 6:00 a.m., Sarah Beth could use the help. After a few minutes, she could see that Sarah Beth had things well under control. She let Tommie take the orders and collect the money while she made the coffees and put them on the pickup counter.

Charles hung around until 6:30 talking with some of his cronies. Linda stood at the bar with her coffee, chatting with her lady friends. They studiously ignored one another. When Charles finally got to the counter to order, he scowled at Tommie. Linda hurried outside the shop and came back in with a sweater. She frequently narrowed her eyes and glared ominously in Tommie's direction, who pretended not to notice. As soon as Charles was served, the two of them sat exactly as Sarah Beth had described, on opposite sides of the table, with eight tables between them, covertly making eye contact while keeping up running conversations with other patrons nearby.

At 6:45, Henry Erving entered Brewster's, escorting Beverly Cantrell. Both Tommie and Sarah Beth were surprised to see them together. Henry was still pale, but he seemed otherwise recovered from his exposure to poison. He put his arm around Beverly's waist and pulled her up to the counter.

"I'll have my usual," he said to Tommie.

"And that would be?" she asked.

He gave her a perplexed look. Realizing she was not Sarah Beth, he clarified his order. "I'll have a large black coffee with two squirts of whipped cream."

"I got it," Sarah Beth called.

"I've never really had a taste for coffee," Beverly said. "I don't even know what to order. Maybe I'll just have water."

"No, I want you to have coffee. You'll like it. I promise. Pick something," he urged.

"I don't know what they are, Henry" she said with a whine.

Henry appeared flustered. "It's coffee, Bev. Do you like things sweet or more bitter?" he asked.

"I sure don't like bitter. Something sweet."

"She'll have a caramel latte with two whips," he ordered, "and give us two of each of those treats back there, please."

Suddenly, the shop got extra busy.

"Hurry up, Henry. Hey, I need a refill on my black and tan, Sarah Beth," Charles said, pushing his way in line behind Beverly.

"Hey, watch it. Other people have to order, you know," a man behind him in line said. "I want four of those bagel bites to go."

"I want a large triple espresso with milk and six kisses," a woman called. "Make it a takeout."

"Make mine a cappuccino, decaf, with three of those bagels," another one said. "For here. No, better get it to go."

"*Salty Sweetheart Mix*, please. Make it two, with two espressos in disposable cups with lids."

Tommie tried valiantly to keep up, but Sarah Beth had to step in and rescue her. "Large black, two whips, in the house. Caramel latte, two whips, in the house. Black and Tan tall, in the house. Triple black and moo, with legs. Unleaded cappu, with legs. Two short blacks, with legs. Coming up," she called, grabbing multiple mugs and filling them quickly. "Tommie, you take care of the food things and man the cash register while I do the drinks."

Tommie was happy to oblige, not knowing the names of the specialty coffees that were being shouted out. She was struck by the difference between coffee drinkers and tea drinkers. Her patrons were relaxed, polite, and courteous. These people were like shoppers at a blue light special trying to be the first ones to get the deals. They jostled each other in line, and Charles bumped Henry, who was holding both his and Beverly's mugs, almost making him spill them.

At 6:50, Finbar entered the shop. Tommie was glad to see him but surprised. When he got to the now empty counter, he ordered a small black coffee. "I took a rideshare here. Thought it would be interesting to see things firsthand."

"It's crazy!" Tommie said. "Too stressful for me. That last bunch of orders was the longest five minutes I've ever spent!"

"Sure, sure. It's what people get used to. Ah, look. There's Henry Erving. He looks to be in much better health today."

"Thanks to you calling him," Tommie said.

"Didn't want him to die on us," Finbar quipped, making his way over to sit at the table adjacent to Henry and Beverly.

"C'mon, Beverly. It should be cool enough now. Just take little sips," Henry said, encouraging Beverly to drink her coffee.

"It's bitter tasting, Henry. I thought it would be sweeter," she said, wrinkling up her nose.

"Here, I've got an idea," he said. He picked the chocolate pieces out of the sweet and salty mix and dropped them in her mug, stirring them with a disposable spoon. "Try it now with the chocolate melted in."

Beverly took a tentative sip and gave a wan smile. "That's a little better. Maybe a bit more sugar?" she said.

Henry hopped up and retrieved three sugar packets from the self-serve counter. She gratefully took them and added all three to her mug. She took another tentative sip.

"It's much better, Henry. That is so gallant of you to wait on me like this."

"Drink up, Bev. We can come here for coffee

together every morning. It'll be fun."

"All right, Henry. If you say so," she agreed, sipping from her oversize mug. A fine sheen of sweat appeared on her upper lip, and her cheeks grew even rosier beneath her makeup.

"Good morning, Miss Cantrell. Henry," Finbar said, raising his eyebrows up and down comically.

"Nice to see you, Finbar. Thank you for calling me yesterday afternoon. I guess I was sicker than I thought," Henry said.

"You were sick yesterday, Henry?" Beverly asked, taking a big swallow of her latte.

"I was. Turns out there was poison in Coral's tea, and I got it on my hands when I was cleaning it up. It made me pretty ill, but I'm all right now," he said.

"That's good," she shook her head slightly. "Henry, would you get me another one of those bagels? I haven't eaten any breakfast, and I worked out hard at the gym this morning. I'm a little lightheaded. I could use some food in my stomach."

"Right away, Bev," he said, going to the counter.

"Miss Cantrell. You do seem a little woozy. Perhaps you're not used to the amount of caffeine there is in coffee. It's more than what's in tea," Finbar said, patting her hand.

"I guess not. I do feel pretty amped up, like doing an aerobic workout."

"Here you go, Bev. Dip it in your coffee. It's

really good that way," Henry suggested.

Beverly complied. She broke the pastry in half and dunked it, then chewed it appreciatively. "It's really good. You're right."

Beverly took two more big swallows of her coffee and slid sideways out of the chair. Finbar grabbed for her arm and caught her just before she landed on the floor. Leaning his head on her chest, he could tell she was not breathing, so he began chest compressions.

Tommie whipped out her cellphone and dialed 9-1-1. She saw several things seemingly at once, like pictures from a slide projector: Sarah Beth was pressed up to the front counter, her eyes wide, her hand to her mouth; Finbar was pushing rhythmically on Beverly's chest while her head lolled to the side; Henry Erving was crumpled across the table in distress; Linda Beadwell and Charles Williams were standing close together in the back by the restroom; and Beverly Cantrell was prostrate on the floor, her eyes staring sightless toward Tommie, her face a bright cherry red.

Chapter Twenty

TOMMIE AND FINBAR sat in two chairs in Brewster's guarding the spot where Beverly Cantrell had lain and where her coffee spilled. The EMTs had already removed her body and transported it to the coroner's office four blocks away. Once again, the lights were on, but the siren was not. It was no surprise; Finbar knew she was dead even as he performed CPR.

Sarah Beth walked back and forth behind the counter shaking her head in distress, a notepad in her hand, trying to recall who had been in the shop for coffee and had left during the one hour in which she had been opened. Tommie could hear her using her own version of barista-speak. "Two blacks, tall, with legs—Sid and Jeanette Spock. Short latte, in the house—Sam Hamilton. Red Eye—Larry Brown. With legs or in the house? I can't remember. Café au Lait, in the house—Linda Beadwell. Short, flat, with legs—that guy with the big mustache, don't know his name. Black and Tan, tall, in the house—Charles Williams. Two Americanos, with legs—Elly James and Jo Clay. Large black, two whips, in the house—Henry Erving. Caramel latte, two whips, in the house—Beverly Cantrell. Black and Tan tall refill, in the house—Charles. Triple black and moo, with legs—Father Duncan. Unleaded cappu, with legs—Louanne Weller. Two short blacks, with legs—Nelson Stone. Short black, in the house—Mr. Holmes."

Henry Erving was still in his seat against the wall, and Charles and Linda had taken chairs across from one another with only two tables in between. When the Police arrived, Earl spotted Tommie and dropped his chin to his chest with a huge sigh, slowly shaking his silver head from side to side.

"Trouble follows you like *Ziggy* with a cloud over his head," he muttered.

Tommie shrugged her shoulders and frowned.

Earl surveyed the room. "Well, well. Hello again, Henry. And you, too, Charles. Who wants to go first?"

Nobody offered, so he selected Finbar.

"I don't believe I've met you, sir. Would you be Ms. Watson's new landlord from Ireland?"

"I am, Officer. My name is Finbar Holmes. How d'you do?"

"I've been much, much better. OK, Mr. Holmes. How about you come with me into the storage room and we'll have a little chat," Earl said, walking toward the back. "All the rest of you stay right where you are. Dale, see to it nobody leaves, blah, blah, blah. You know the drill. Jenny, you come on into the storeroom with me as a witness like last time, so I'm not alone with anyone."

Tommie sat woodenly, carefully avoiding the coffee on the floor and the table. She flexed her toes, wishing she had something on which to prop her leg. After a few minutes, Finbar and Earl returned. Tommie raised her hand.

"Ms. Watson. Come on in here. Let's get you taken care of," Earl said. His face reflected frustration at seeing her in the midst of yet another crime scene. *Guess I'll have to cross Earl off my list of dating prospects,* Tommie thought as she entered the storeroom.

While she was being questioned by the policeman and his partner, Finbar kept an eye on the suspects in the coffee shop. Henry seemed to be in shock. His face was pale, and he was breathing raggedly. Finbar was afraid he had been in contact with the poison again.

"Henry, did you touch Miss Cantrell's coffee either before or after she spilled it?" he asked, keeping his voice quiet.

"No. Made that mistake already. Wouldn't do it again. Glad I didn't take a sip, though. Wish I hadn't brought her in here, Finbar, but I thought I could make a go of it with her, since Coral's gone. But now, Beverly's gone, too. Maybe I'm a jinx when it comes to women."

"Coral was the one you went for?"

"I liked Beverly."

"But she wasn't yer girlfriend, was she Henry?"

"Not yet, but she would have been. She really liked me."

"It was Coral you wanted, though. She's the one you were watching when she came in Watson's."

"I wasn't stalking her, Holmes. I was just watching her."

"Sure, sure, I understand. So sorry, Henry."

Tommie exited the storeroom, and Charles went in with Earl. Finbar caught Tommie's eye when she came back and sat down beside him.

"Missus, yer foot must be hurting. I see you limping. Here, put it up on this chair." He moved it closer to her, helping her lift the heavy boot onto the seat.

"Hey, Earl said to stay put," Dale warned.

"I'm not going anywhere, young man. Ms. Watson needed to elevate her ankle. I'm just taking the chair behind her," Finbar explained.

The change of seating put him closer to Linda.

"Halloo, Mrs. Beadwell. I remember you from the Bingo. We had to leave early. How did you do?"

"I won a couple," she replied tersely.

"Good on you. I could tell you had a foolproof system going there. Maybe I can go again, and you can teach me the finer points. I'd very much like to get the paper cards and a stamper like what yerself had."

Linda responded favorably to his flattery despite

her dislike for Tommie. She gave him a smile that almost seemed to touch her eyes.

"I'd like that, Mr. Holmes, *if* you happen to come by yourself some night," she said, making it clear she wanted no part of Tommie Watson's company.

"Right. 'Tis a date for sure then, lass. And perhaps, you'll introduce me to yer leprechaun. I may well bring himself a tiny pot of gold." He winked, and she giggled in response.

"Terrible thing, this what's happened to Miss Cantrell. What d'you make of it?" he asked.

"I don't know. Mrs. Brewster's shop has always been very clean. I will tell you one thing, though, Mr. Holmes," she said leaning in closer to him and speaking in a hushed voice. "I stepped out to my car to get my sweater about 6:40, and on my way in, I heard Beverly arguing with Henry. She didn't *want* to have coffee. Said she *hated* it. He *made* her come in and *drink* that coffee." She sat back just as the door opened, and Charles came out of the storeroom.

"Mrs. Beadwell, I'd like to talk to you now, please," Earl said, ushering her into the storeroom.

While Linda was in with Earl and Jenny, Charles sat at the table pulling on his thin mustache and glaring at everyone else in the room. Finbar took the opportunity to speak with him.

"Halloo, Charlie. We seem to keep seeing one another. What an active town this turns out to be,"

Finbar said.

"It's not usually like this, Mr. Holmes. I'm sorry you've arrived when everything seems to be so screwed up," Charles admitted.

"From what you tell me, this shop proprietor has good hygiene practices. Is that not what you said yesterday?"

"Well, normally, I'd say so. But now, I'm wondering if her equipment needs upgrading as well."

"Sure, it could be that, or it could be someone is on a killing spree."

"Exactly what are you implying, Holmes?" Charles glowered.

Finbar leaned in closer. "That lad up there. He has ties with both the dead women. What d'you make of that, Charlie?"

"You could be right, Holmes. Jilted lover, maybe? Don't know why he'd kill his newest squeeze, though. That's a waste."

"Maybe he was not so interested in Miss Cantrell. Maybe she was making demands on him. Maybe even blackmail?"

"Who said anything about blackmail? I'm sure Beverly wouldn't have a reason to blackmail anyone, for crying out loud. Though, I have to admit, she was a shark, and I wouldn't put it past her. You don't know what kind of illegal things those UPS employees ship back and forth," he said, tapping his mustache with his finger.

"Weapons, stolen merchandise, drugs. Who knows? And that Coral Beadwell was well known for opening up other people's mail and packages."

"That's right. Ms. Watson said she thought one of yer packages had been damaged by the woman."

"That wasn't the only one she opened. She was a hateful, spiteful, conniving woman."

"D'you think Mr. Erving was in on the scheme to fence stolen merchandise?"

"Wouldn't surprise me in the least, and maybe Bev knew it and confronted him."

"But Miss Cantrell, she seemed to be a nice woman. Well put together, if you know what I mean? What would she see in that Mr. Erving? Pardon me, but he's no Charles Williams, is he?"

"That's for damn sure."

"Sometimes 'tis a curse to be attractive, eh?"

Charles cast his eyes toward the storeroom and back at Holmes. "Yep," he said with an evil grin and squinted eyes, "sometimes it can be a real curse."

"All right, Henry. Let's have you now," Earl said when Linda finished her meeting with him. Henry moved toward the back slowly, as though in a daze, and disappeared into the storeroom.

There was a knock on the front door, and Dale opened it to the same two gloved technicians that had processed Tommie's shop. They carefully retrieved the broken coffee mug and used soft white cloths to absorb the liquid on the table and the floor. They took pictures of the entire shop, as well as where the people were sitting. Tommie, Charles, and Henry had already been printed, so the techs printed Sarah Beth, Linda, and Holmes. Then, they began dusting the shop surfaces with black fingerprint powder.

Earl released Henry and walked back into *Brewster's,* nodding to the techs.

"Sarah Beth, I'm going to need you to stay behind and talk with me. Everyone else, you can go home, but don't leave town. Stick around, because I'm sure I'll have more questions," Earl said, fixing Tommie with a meaningful stare.

Charles and Linda moved to the back door where Jenny was standing guard, and Henry walked to the front. Finbar helped Tommie stand and escorted her toward the back. As they reached the open end of the counter area, Tommie made a beeline into the U and shoved past Sarah Beth. She hobbled up to the back counter and grabbed a *Besame Bagel Bite,* a couple of *Double Sweet Kisses,* and a handful of the *Salty Sweetheart Mix.*

"Just in case any of you have doubts about the treats I made, here's to you!" she said, putting all of them in her mouth at once. She chewed and swallowed and stared at the open-mouthed group inside Brewster's Coffee Shoppe.

"Happy Valentine's Day to all!" she quipped.

Chapter Twenty-One

ZED AND RED were happy to have Tommie home, even though she could tell they hadn't moved from the bed where she left them earlier that morning. She opened the back door and let them frolic around the yard with Sherlock while she sat huddled in the Adirondack chair with her eyes closed. Finbar pulled one of his dinette chairs outside and placed it on the uncovered part of the cement patio in the sun. Neither of them talked; they just sat while the dogs played happily in the grass. It was Finbar who eventually broke the silence.

"Missus?"

"Hmm?"

"This was none of yer doing. Nobody knew you'd be there at Mrs. Brewster's shop. This is something else entirely."

"How so?"

"Who was the target?"

"Beverly."

"No, I don't think so."

"Was it Sarah Beth? It wasn't me this time, I'm pretty sure."

Finbar sat contemplating an ant making its way across the concrete carrying a leaf of grass. He shook his head slowly and crossed his legs, his hand to his chin. Then, he got up and went into the house. When he returned, the calabash pipe was in his mouth.

"Thomasina. We've missed something. I'm not sure what, but our investigation is flawed.

Tommie was tired, but he was in the mood to puzzle. "What's missing?" she asked with a deep sigh.

"Motive. Always motive. Who had reason to kill both Coral Beadwell and Beverly Cantrell?"

"Besides me? I don't know."

"Think, lad. Let's talk this through."

"Oh, Finbar. I'm so tired. I've been up since 5:00, another person has died gruesomely in my presence, and I just want to shut down and decompress. Let's leave it for today, OK? I ... I just can't think." She was dangerously close to tears again, so he backed off. At least he backed off talking about it. His mind, however, would not quit.

"Ah, sure. Why don't you go in and lie down on yer bed and put on a film?" He pronounced it "fil-em," but she was too exhausted to even smile at him. "I'll keep the lads with me, whilst you have a rest, maybe even a nap.

When you feel like it, come 'round, and I'll feed you. How does that sound?"

Tommie smiled with her lips closed and nodded, grateful for the chance to sink into oblivion for a little while. He helped her up from the chair and escorted her to her house, patting her on the back awkwardly before she pulled the door shut. Taking the dining chair back inside, he grabbed his legal pads and returned to the yard, taking a seat in the blue resin chair. As the dogs laid on the grass soaking up the sunshine, and Tommie queued up a movie (he heard it though the wall of her bedroom), Finbar worked his magic with the legal pads.

Four hours later, Tommie awoke with a start. Taking a glance at the clock, she was surprised to see it was noon. She sat up in the bed, wondering where her dogs were, and then she remembered what her mind had blessedly blocked out while she slept: Beverly Cantrell was murdered that day.

Tommie groggily limped to the bathroom, splashed her face with water, and brushed her teeth. She ran a brush through her disheveled hair and put on a fresh pair of scrubs. Then, she went out the kitchen door and walked to Finbar's.

"Haloo, here's yer missus, boys. You look better, Thomasina. C'mon in. I'm just finishing up from peeling and boiling these spuds for our lunch. I'll let them steam for a bit with the cabbage, and we can have a lovely meal of *colcannon*. Take yer seat on the sofa. The afghan's there waiting."

Tommie dutifully took her place on the couch and propped her leg on the blanket, dropping her hand to pet her dogs, who were happy for the attention but happier to curl up on the floor with Sherlock. She could see the notepads on Finbar's side table, full of writing. He had been busy.

"Have you solved it?" she asked.

"Not altogether, but I've made a right dent in it. I'll tell you more in just a minute. Let me just put a lid on the pot."

Holmes came over and took his seat, the pipe hanging on his lip. He picked up the legal pads and laid them on his lap. "Thomasina, whilst the lunch is steaming, I think we'll do a little question and answer between the two of us and see what we can uncover in our minds, if yer up to it."

"I feel much better, thank you."

"Would you like a sup of tea before we begin? I'm having a cold Guinness. You can have one as well, if you'd prefer."

"I'd just like some water right now, but I can get it. You get organized." She got to her feet and went to the kitchen. Taking a washed glass from the dish drainer, she filled it with water and resumed her seat. "Ready for the Q & A."

"Right, then. I've written down some questions, and let's see if we can answer them. I'll be the scribe. First, two related questions: Why would someone want to murder Coral Beadwell? What was it about her that made her the killer's target?"

"OK. I'm assuming you want me to answer in terms of each of our main suspects."

"Yes. In the order we interviewed them, please."

"OK. Sarah Beth. The only thing I can say is that she was very angry that Coral convinced the Ladies' Charity Organization from Trinity Episcopal Church to have their monthly meetings at Watson's. She told me she felt betrayed because she went to the same church with Coral and was in the LCO. Coral taking business away from her from among her own friends was really pretty cold hearted."

"Sure, it was. Go on."

"Henry. Unrequited love. Coral rebuffed him and humiliated him in front of others. Revenge. Coral engineered the promotion for herself that Henry deserved. Beverly. She was jealous of Henry's obsession with Coral. But that's kind of a moot point now that she's been killed, too."

"True. It does put a kink in our theories. How about Charlie?"

"Ugh. Charles. He had a beef with Coral because of the way she treated him at the UPS Store. He's used to being kowtowed to, and she didn't do it. Also, she had been opening his mail and packages. He said so himself, didn't he? I wonder what he was getting in those packages that Coral found interesting enough to damage and blatantly snoop into?"

"I don't know, but that may be a key detail we need to find out. Linda Beadwell?"

"Greed. She wanted that historic house, and the only way she could get it was for Coral to die. That's a fact! Plus, she has a fling going with Charles. If Don Lareby and his sisters knew about the affair, and Sarah Beth also knew, then I guaran-dang-tee Coral Beadwell knew! I wouldn't be surprised if she was blackmailing both Charles and her sister-in-law."

"Yes. That's an excellent observation, lad. Brilliant deduction. OK. Why would the killer use cyanide poison?"

"Hmm. That's a little trickier. Poison is fairly easy to obtain, and it's not immediately evident, not like a stabbing or a shooting."

"Did you know poison is more likely to be used by a woman than a man?" Finbar asked.

"No, I didn't. Why is that?"

"It's fast acting, efficient, and it's almost certainly successful in the right dosage. Plus, it can be administered anonymously. The murderer need not be present for it to be effective, and one need not be face to face with the victim, which is a method more common amongst male killers. They're usually more violent."

"Those are good points. But think of this: couldn't a man use it to cast suspicion on a woman for the same reason?"

"Oh, ho! Now yer thinking, missus. That lets none of our suspects off the hook. Good on you."

"I have my moments. What's next?" She was beginning to get her second wind.

"Who had access to Coral? What insured she would be the victim?" he asked.

"Sarah Beth has a key to the adjoining door. She could come in anytime she wanted and tamper with the cups on the counter."

"Yes, but what how could she be sure Coral got the poison instead of someone else?"

"Oh, yeah. I see what you mean. Hmm. Henry worked with Coral at the UPS Store. If he'd had his fill of her mean treatment, couldn't he have put the poison on something that she handled daily, like stuff on her desk? He wouldn't have necessarily had to put it in her cup," she reasoned, "and Coral could've transferred it to the cup inadvertently when she added sugar or squeezed her lemon."

"That's a possibility. And then afterwards, cleaning up the mess gave him just enough poison in his system to make him sick and to take suspicion off himself," he suggested.

"Oh, that's true. Now, Beverly, once again. Do we back off of her as a suspect because she was killed?"

"For now. Let's go to Charlie-boy," Finbar said.

"You really ticked him off by calling him

Charlie," she laughed. "He was livid."

"Of course. That's why I did it, to get a rise out of him. It's elementary, Watson. When people get angry, they slip up, and he did. We know he touched Coral's cup, so that's his access to her."

"And Linda was her sister-in-law and lived right next door, so there was plenty of access. Plus, she was in the shop that day when I was in the window. She knew where my cups were stored, even though she'd never been in there before."

"That brings me to the poisoning itself. I want you to consider several questions. First, who had access to yer shop, and who had access to the cups and could make sure Coral got the poisoned one?"

"I think I answered that. Sarah Beth, Charles, and Linda all had been in the shop at one time or another. Charles, and probably Linda, touched the cups on that day. I actually saw him put his hands on her cup. And Beverly touched them, too, but she doesn't count now. Henry was never in until after Coral died. Anyone who frequented the shop when Coral was there knew she had a favorite cup. Don and his sisters knew, but I don't know if Charles did."

"And Sarah Beth?"

"I don't recall if we ever discussed that. Coral was not really a topic of my conversations with Sarah Beth since the charity group thing. I didn't want to rub salt in the wound, you know? And Henry doesn't figure in for that question either. But Linda? She may have been aware because, like the sisters said, Coral was a creature of habit, and Linda surely knew it."

"Thomasina, we know the cup was tainted, but what if you hadn't given Coral that particular cup? Did she ever drink from another?"

"I always gave her that cup, Finbar, unless it had gotten dirty or something. When she was running late, though, sometimes she'd have a cold tea from the cooler."

"So, she might just as likely have drunk from a different cup. Is that possible?"

"Yes. It's certainly possible, if I had a busy day, and if her cup was still been in the dishwasher from the night before. Instead of waiting, she drank from another jumbo cup. That did happen occasionally. Do you have another theory?"

"I'm thinking, in light of Beverly's demise in the coffee shop, that it's possible Coral was not the intended victim. In fact, I'm thinking there may have been no intended victim at either shop."

"You've lost me."

"What if the *victim* was not who was important? What if the *location* was what was important?"

"The location … instead of the person? That puts a whole new spin on things. That would mean my *shop* was the target. Is that what you're getting at?"

"That is exactly what I mean. Who benefits if you go out of business?"

"Wow. Charles Williams, for sure. He wants to buy my shop ... *and* Sarah Beth's, and even though it's a family property and can't be sold, Sanderson would let Charles have a long-term lease on it. Oh, my gosh. The second murder in Sarah Beth's shop could be to drive *her* out of business!" Her jaw dropped as she considered the ramifications. "Charles ... and Linda by association. They would both benefit from Watson's and Brewster's going out of business."

"What are the odds of two women, both tied to Henry Erving by the way, turning up dead in two different shops by the same method—poison in and on the cups. I'll bet yer cousin the coroner will confirm the same cause of death for Beverly as was for Coral. You'll have to ring him up tomorrow. But just so we don't get ahead of ourselves, we need to be systematic about other possibilities, as well."

"All right, but I'm still betting on it being Charles and Linda."

"Nevertheless, we need to be more certain. Can't go about throwing the finger at people just because we dislike them. Right? After you speak with yer cousin tomorrow, we'll discuss Beverly's murder. For now, let's take a rest and have some lunch. I have a throat from talking, and there's spuds to mash. Come to the table. I'll have it ready right quick," he said.

Tommie watched as Finbar mashed the potatoes with a huge chunk of Irish butter and then folded in the drained and chopped cabbage. The *colcannon* he placed in a bowl before her was fragrant and savory, and she ate every bit, noisily scraping her bowl to get the last of it.

"Finbar, that was delicious. I guess I better take my mutts on home before they believe they live here. I think I'll have cereal for supper and make it an early night. See you in the morning," she said while he put the dishes into the sink to soak. As she walked toward the door, he stopped her with a hand on her arm.

"Thomasina, I have a nagging thought I need to resolve before I can sleep tonight," he said.

"What's that?" she asked.

"You said it was possible Ms. Beadwell could have chosen another cup to drink from. Did that happen very often?"

"No, not often. But sometimes it did."

"And she chose from the teacup caddy?"

"No, almost never. She was funny that way. If she couldn't have her special cup, I let her use my cup."

"*Yer* cup? What d'you mean, *yer* cup?"

"I have a jumbo cup I usually drink from. It's similar to hers, only mine's teal and white instead of teal and yellow, and mine has a picture of Zed and Red on one side. Coral's had a cat."

"And where d'you keep yer cup, missus?"

"On the counter by the caddies … right next to Coral's cup."

Finbar stared at her in shock, and she stared back.

"Thomasina, what if it was *yer* cup the killer had poisoned, and not hers?" he asked quietly. "Then, *you* would be the one who's dead right now."

"But, I'm not, Finbar. First of all, my teacup wasn't poisoned. And secondly, even if someone had tampered with it, I have a policy to never drink tea while I have customers in the shop. I drink bottled water."

Tommie smiled, and because his face was so stricken, she impulsively stepped forward and kissed him on the cheek.

"So, get some sleep, lad. It's been a bugger of a day for both of us!"

Chapter Twenty-Two

EARL PETRY called the next morning at 8:00. Tommie was well rested from an uneventful, dreamless night's sleep. Seeing his name on the caller ID, she answered the call brightly.

"My, but you're a chipper one today," he said, his smooth voice getting her undivided attention.

"Hi, Earl. I drank a nighttime tea and had a blissful eight hours of rest, for a change," she reported.

"I'm happy to hear that, Tommie. You've had quite a shocking week. I wanted to call again and see how you're holding up, and I wanted to let you know that your shop's been processed and released as a crime scene. You can officially go back in there."

"Oh, Earl! That's the best news ever. Does that mean I'm no longer a person of interest?"

He chuckled. "In one sense, yes. In another sense, you're still a person of interest ... to me."

Tommie was surprised at the admission and held her tongue for once.

"Tommie? You still there?" he asked.

"Uh, yes. I'm here. I ... wow. Thanks, Earl. That really means a lot to me, especially in light of all the trouble I've been to you lately."

"It means a lot that your shop's cleared or that you're a person of interest?"

"Both," she admitted, suddenly feeling shy and unsure of herself.

Evidently, Earl was, as well. "So, that's all, then. You can go back to your shop. But, Tommie, please don't go into Sarah Beth's store. We're still processing it."

"OK. I promise I'll stay out," she said. "By the way, can you tell me anything about Beverly's death? I haven't talked to Sanderson."

"Yet," he scoffed. "Off the record, no, I can't tell you anything. How about you tell me what you think?" His tone had softened.

"Okie dokie. Will you confirm it if I'm right?"

"We'll see. I can't make any promises to you. But try me."

"Beverly died of the same cyanide-type poisoning as Coral. You'll find a lethal dose of it in her coffee mug."

"And you know this how?"

"She fell out just like Coral did, and her face was bright red, just like Coral's."

"That sounds reasonable. What else?" He was

being deliberately noncommittal, but that was understandable because of his position, and also because Earl Petry didn't generally say more than was necessary. That he called her a person of interest to him spoke volumes to Tommie. She had to trust him.

"Earl, if I share my suspicions with you, will you keep me in the loop? I've done a little investigating and research on my own, and I have some theories."

"I know you have, Tommie." His sigh was loud and heavy. "You shouldn't be doing your own investigating. That could be dangerous. Someone has killed two women in less than a week. Do you really think you meddling is wise? You could be the next target."

"I realize that, and I'm not so sure I haven't been a target all along."

"Because?" His voice was a tiny bit alarmed.

"Because of what I've found out. And ..."

"Tommie.? Tell me what you think you know."

"This may sound far-fetched and a little paranoid but hear me out. Coral was particular about certain things, like she always drank from the same cup. And if it wasn't available to her, she drank from mine, which looks almost exactly like hers and is kept in the same place I kept hers. The poison was in *her* cup, but it could just as easily have been put in *my* cup, but it wasn't, so that's a good thing," she blurted.

"Yes."

"And Charles Williams is such a greedy, hateful

man to me *and* to Sarah Beth. He wants *both* of our shops. And he and Coral had already been in an argument that *I* witnessed because she was opening his packages. Who knows *what* he's been receiving? He threatened Coral at the table, *and* he's having an affair with Linda Beadwell, and *she* was in my shop that Monday and could've contaminated *any* of the cups. And she told Mr. Holmes that Henry *made* Bev drink that poisoned coffee. And *everybody* piles lies on top of lies, so *who* can you *believe?*" She was out of breath by the time she finished.

Earl was quiet for a little while before he spoke again, but when he did, his tone was emphatic.

"Tommie. Stop doing your own investigation. I can't stress that enough. Go to your shop, clean it up, restock your products, do inventory, make a potion. I don't care what you do, but please do something boring and mundane. I couldn't bear it if you were harmed. Do you understand me, Darlin'? Stop playing detective. That's my job. OK? Can you do that for me, please?"

"Yes," she said. Her voice was small and timid to her ears and sounded like it came from a different person.

"Thank you. I'll tell you what. What you know and what you even suspect, you can tell me. I'm very impressed with your investigative instincts. I just don't want you to put yourself in danger. Be an armchair detective, if you want. But let me do the legwork. All right, Tommie? And stay away from anybody you have pegged as a suspect."

"OK, Earl. I will. Thanks for releasing my shop. I have plenty of work to do there. I appreciate everything, and I'm glad I'm a person of interest … to you."

"You are. I'll keep in touch, Tommie. Goodbye."

Tommie Watson ate the last few bites of her peanut butter and strawberry jam sandwich and downed the rest of her morning Rooibos tea with blue agave syrup. *A person of interest,* she thought with a smile. *I like that.*

Zed and Red trotted into the kitchen and went directly to the back door. Tommie heard Sherlock scratching and opened it so her boys could run out and play with their buddy. Putting her cup and plate into the sink, she walked outside and knocked on Finbar's door.

"Haloo, missus. How did you sleep?" he asked.

"Wonderfully," she reported.

"And myself as well. Are you ready for some sleuthing today? It's Friday, and our two favorite suspects should be at work. I'd like to talk with Henry a bit and Charlie," he said.

"Oh, OK. Earl called and said I can go back to my shop, so I thought maybe I'd do a little cleaning."

"Lovely. I'll help you. Just give me a moment to spiff up." He rinsed his dishes and grabbed a small soft-sided cooler. "I'm taking a few Guinness with me, for myself and Henry, and maybe one for Charlie. See if I can loosen their tongues."

"That's great. While you're talking with them,

I'll just stay at the shop, if that's all right."

"Sure. That's a fine idea. No sense yer being around whilst I try to talk man to man. No offense, but Henry's on the shy side, and Charlie hates you. Maybe we can ring up the lads at the bank and meet them at their sandwich shop for lunch and gossip, eh?"

Tommie smiled broadly, and though she had promised Earl she would not do any investigating, she had made no such promise for Finbar. "Meet me at the car in 15 minutes. Zed! Red! Come on, boys. Mom's gotta go to work."

The dogs understood the word "work" perfectly and came trotting back in. She gave each of them four Vienna Sausages as treats and exited the front door.

Chapter Twenty-Three

FINBAR HOLMES got Tommie settled on her stool in the shop, and she started cleaning the counters with a spray bottle solution of alcohol and peroxide. While she shuffled around and scrubbed the fingerprint powder off all the surfaces, he got a broom from the storeroom and went to work sweeping the powder from the floors. Using a wet-jet mop, he mopped the entire shop twice, including the bathroom and the storage room. As the two of them worked, they discussed questions and answers regarding Beverly's death.

"I don't have my pad, but I'll remember and can transfer it to our interview checklist when we get home. First thing we need to discuss: why would someone want to kill Beverly? What about her made her a victim?" Holmes asked.

"From what I can tell, Henry didn't really want Beverly; he wanted Coral all along. Maybe he thought Bev was the one who caused Coral's death?"

"That's an interesting theory. Revenge, then?"

"Could be. Now, Charles. We know he had to split his commission for the Beadwell House with Beverly. 'His Greediness' wouldn't like that happening a second time. Also, and I thought about this last night, maybe Beverly knew about his affair with Linda and threatened him. She could've said something like if he didn't give her more than half the commission, she would tell Linda's husband about them."

"That could be a very strong motive for Charlie to kill her. The money. And even motive for Linda. I'm sure she wouldn't want her husband to know about their illicit dalliance.

"Their illicit dalliance? Somehow it doesn't sound so seedy when you phrase it like that. Anyway, I think maybe there's more to that damaged package deal than we realize. I bet you a dollar to a donut Beverly knew what was in the package ... or packages."

"Oh, missus. That's definitely a theory I need to check up on when I visit the men after lunch. I can ask Henry. I bet he knows ... if not what was in them parcels, then maybe where they come from. I can agitate Charlie-boy again and see if he makes a mistake in what he tells me. Yer brilliant."

"Elementary, my dear Holmes. Now, as far as Linda Beadwell is concerned, I think it's possible Beverly *was* blackmailing her, and Linda needed to shut her up.

You saw her temper the other night at Bingo. Also, whatever benefits Charles benefits Linda."

"Righto. And how about yer friend Sarah Beth?"

"Crap. I keep forgetting about her. I can't see why she would kill someone in her own shop and have the blame pointed at her. That's like sabotaging yourself."

"Not if she did it to point blame *away* from her."

"How do you figure, Finbar?"

"She might have wanted to point the blame to someone else, like Charlie. The 'I'm a victim, too' defense. Misdirection, my dear Watson. Misdirection."

"Hmph. I think it's reaching, but we'll consider it. For that matter, *I* could've done it to point blame away from me! You know, like 'oh look, somebody's been killed in a different shop.' Makes me look less guilty."

"Ah, sure. But point of fact is you did not kill the first victim, Thomasina. And whilst we're talking about how things appear, I have to tell you that stuffing those confections into yer mouth like you did was sheer genius. Who would ever take you for a murderer? Mental, maybe, but not a murderer."

Tommie burst out laughing. "It was crazy wasn't it? I don't know why I did it. Guess I just snapped. Should've seen your face … everyone's faces, for that matter. Priceless."

"All right, missus. Here is the million Euro question: How could the killer be sure Beverly Cantrell got the tainted mug and swallowed the poison?"

"That is the question, isn't it? Who even knew she would be in the coffee shop? I was certainly surprised to see her walk in. She was a regular tea customer at my shop. When Henry brought Beverly in, I was speechless … and you know that's unusual for me."

"Quite true, on all accounts. The only person who could possibly know Beverly would be drinking coffee was Henry. He brought her in. You said he ordered for her, and he encouraged her to drink. I hate to say it because I like the lad, but that puts him squarely in the crosshairs, so to speak."

"Finbar, you told me Linda vehemently alluded to him as having poisoned Bev," Tommie said, moving over to spray and wipe down all the drink bottles in the small coolers.

"She did. She very *emphatically* incriminated Henry to me and probably Officer Petry as well."

"Why did she have such contempt toward Henry, I wonder. Could it be he *does* know something illegal she and Charles are trying to hide. Maybe about those packages? I'll be interested to hear what you find out from him."

"Quite. Let's go back to the question of access. All of them had access to Brewster's Coffee Shoppe and to the mugs. You said yerself it got so busy before I arrived you couldn't keep up. Anything could have happened during that time that neither you nor Sarah Beth would notice," Holmes said.

"Multiple people touched that mug, Finbar. Multiple people. Sarah Beth, Charles, Henry, Linda, and even me," Tommie acknowledged.

"It takes us back to the question: how could the killer be sure that Beverly got the tainted mug?"

"I don't know, Finbar. She wasn't a regular, and she didn't have a special mug like Coral."

They were silent for a few minutes as they mulled over that fact. Then Finbar spoke again. "Did Sarah Beth have her own mug like you did?"

"No. She didn't. She always used a disposable cup for herself so she could throw it away. Why?"

"I'm hoping to eliminate both you and her from being the killer's targets. I hope nobody wants the two of you dead."

"Oh, yeah," she muttered. "That idea really sucks for us."

"Quite. So, Thomasina. We must explore what we discussed last night. What if it was not the *victim* who was important? What if was the *location* that was important? Who benefits if you and Sarah Beth both go out of business?"

"Charles Williams," she growled. It keeps coming back to Charles Williams and his greed, and Linda Beadwell is guilty by association, and maybe as an accomplice to murder."

"I believe you are correct, Thomasina. The only way it works for both shops to be targeted and for any of the other suspects—yerself included—to be considered guilty is if the poisoning was done as deflection to cast suspicion on someone else. Which would you say is the stronger motive?"

"Greed," they said simultaneously.

Tommie glanced at the huge wall clock and noticed the time. "Oh my gosh, Finbar, it's already 11:45! If you want to have lunch with the Lareby siblings and pump them for more gossip, I need to hurry and give Don Lareby a call."

"Yes, let's arrange to meet them at noon. You remember the name of the establishment? Something outer space-related, I believe."

"Yes. The Lunch Pad. Calling now. Oh, hello. May I speak to Don Lareby, please? Thanks. Hi, Don. It's Tommie Watson. Oh yeah, just fine. Listen, Mr. Holmes and I were wondering if you and your sisters would like to meet us at The Lunch Pad for lunch at 12:00? You would? Great. We'll see you there and hold a table. OK. Bye." She ended the call and checked the clock again. "All right, Finbar. It's a date. We have just enough time to wash up and drive over."

Tommie was excited to hear the thoughts (no, the out and out gossip) from the Lareby siblings. She convinced herself that, since they were not suspects, it was not really investigating, so she would still be keeping her promise to Earl.

Chapter Twenty-Four

THE LUNCH PAD was little more than a hole in the wall with a themed décor. As soon as they entered, Tommie was able to see Finbar in full Irish food inspector mode. He swept his eyes all around the diner and took in the floors, the walls, the table settings, and the service staff. They were led to a round table that sat six, and napkin-wrapped cutlery was deposited at each place setting, along with laminated menus.

Finbar smiled at the waitress who brought them glasses of ice water and attempted to look pleasant.

"Lass, could you bring us several more napkins and an additional glass of water with no ice and some lemons, please?" he asked.

When the waitress returned, he thanked her, then he immediately squeezed four lemon wedges into the water. He took two napkins and dipped them into the lemon water glass. After carefully, but vigorously wiping the table at both his and Tommie's place, he dried the areas with more napkins and pushed them to the side. Then, he repeated the process with the silverware and the menus before depositing all the used napkins into the glass of lemon water. He signaled the girl, and when she came over, he handed her the glass.

"I'm very sorry. We had a spill," he managed.

"No problem. Ready to order yet?"

"No, we are waiting for some others. Oh, here they are. Please give us a few moments." He waved at Don and the sisters, and they joined them at the table.

"I'm so glad you called, Tommie," Don said.

"Yes, we are. How are you, Mr. Holmes, I mean Finbar," Susan said with a giggle.

"Quite well, lass. And the two of ye're lookin' lovely as ever. Tell me what's tasty in this place." The exaggerated accent was back strong as before as the space suited waitress waited to take their orders.

"I like the *Rocket Rueben with Meteor Mustard.* It's especially tangy, and the pickles are nice and crisp," Elaine said.

"It's the *Full Moon Swiss Cheese Melt* for me," Susan said, "with the *Venus Vegetables of the Day.*"

"I always get the same thing—the *French Big Dipper* with a side of *Sputnik Spuds.* They're really French fries," he confided to Finbar.

"How about you, missus Thomasina. What catches yer fancy?" Finbar asked with raised eyebrows.

"I believe I will have the *Satellite Salad with Crater Croutons*," she said, trying valiantly not to laugh. *And I thought my food names were funny.*

"So many choices. I shall try the *Orbit Omelet with Hubble Ham*. Sounds lovely. Great place you've picked out."

"We like it—especially the novel names Sid and Jeanette Spock give to all the dishes. It's so clever," Elaine said.

"So, tell me Finbar, I hear there was some excitement at Brewster's Coffee Shoppe yesterday. Another murder," Don said, "and on the heels of the other one right next door."

"Yes, it seems Miss Beverly Cantrell got hold of poisoned coffee. What d'you make of that?" Finbar replied.

"Something fishy about it. You know she's a tea drinker, don't you Tommie. She's been in your shop lots of times. Why on earth would she get coffee?" Susan remarked.

"Because of our Henry Erving, Sister. And him just coming off of his obsession with Coral Beadwell," Elaine said.

"Do you think he did it?" Tommie asked.

"Not me. I think Charles Williams and Linda Beadwell had a hand in that one," Susan said.

"Why?" Tommie asked.

"To keep from splitting that huge commission,

of course."

"But Sister, how did they know she would be there?" Elaine asked. "Henry's the only one who knew. He brought her and ordered her coffee."

"But why would Henry kill Bev?" Tommie asked.

"To get back at her for killing Coral. I think it's possible Beverly got rid of Coral so she could make hoo-hoo with Henry."

"But to murder her?" Tommie prompted.

"No, no, no. You're both wrong," Don said. "It was Charles and Linda for sure. They needed to shut Beverly up."

"About what?" Finbar asked.

"About the affair, for one thing. Coral and Beverly both knew about it. And to cover up his little side business. They both knew about that, too."

"Side business?" Finbar questioned.

Don and his sisters looked at one another, and then the three of them leaned in closer to the table and lowered their voices dramatically.

"Charles Williams has a side business going. Pharmaceuticals. He gets weekly deliveries at the UPS Store. Coral—we know she was a snoopy woman—she 'damaged' packages when she wanted to see what was in them. Charles caught her doing it. She knew what he was getting every week," Don said.

"She threatened to tell if he didn't throw some extra cash her way," Susan said.

"No!" Tommie exclaimed.

"Yes! Beverly knew, too. She had a bag of something that was in one of Charles' packages hidden in her locked desk drawer. Henry gave it to her. Drugs," Elaine said.

"Why would Charlie be getting drugs every week?" Finbar asked.

"I heard from a guy in my poker group that he supplies a cousin or a nephew in another city who sells them and splits the profit with Charles."

"What kind? Heroin? Cocaine?" Finbar asked.

"No, prescription meds, like Ritalin, Celexa, Prozac, and Adderall. The kids buy them up like crazy," Don said.

"I'm in shock," Tommie said.

"And did you know that Linda Beadwell's husband is a pharmacist? That's right. He runs the Floribunda Rx-All. I would not be surprised if he's getting some of those 'discount' designer drugs, too," Susan said.

"I did not know that," Tommie admitted. "A pharmacist, huh? What are those drugs used for?"

"College kids take them to get high or to help them study. Ritalin and Adderall keep them awake. They're legal amphetamines for children with ADHD to slow them down. Works differently in people with attention deficit," Don said.

"And Celexa is for depression. So is *Prozac.* It's

also an adult medication for OCD," Elaine said.

"I know what Tylenol is, and that's about it. They gave me something from the hospital for the broken ankle pain that was really strong, but it caused me to have respiratory distress," Tommie said.

"Oohh. That sounds like Ultracet. You don't want to take that. Powerful stuff," Elaine confirmed.

"Yeah, I remember. But how do you know all that?"

"My first husband was a psychiatrist, so he prescribed them," Elaine admitted.

"And my second husband was a pharmacist, so he dispensed them," Susan said.

"And my daughter told me a lot of the high school and college kids take meds for various mental and emotional disorders, and so do a lot of adults around here," Don said. "My poker buddies told me about some of them. Thomas Beadwell's daughter in college from his first marriage has OCD—obsessive compulsive disorder. She takes Prozac. Gary Brewster takes Haldol for bipolar disorder, and his son takes Celexa for his depression. I think Charles could have been their supplier, but I can't say for sure. I can't begin to tell you all the people on Opioids! Beverly Cantrell took some kind of an amphetamine for weight loss."

"That's phentermine," Susan said. "Sister and I took it long years ago with fenfluramine. They called it fen-phen. We didn't know at the time it could damage your heart. Live and learn the hard way, huh?"

"Yes, and I'd rather be a living pudgy woman than a dead skinny one," Elaine said, and both sisters erupted in laughter.

The food arrived, and the five of them ate quickly with sporadic conversation. Afterwards, Finbar picked up the check and left a generous tip, which delighted Don and impressed the sisters even more with him. They parted, promising to do it another time, and the two amateur sleuths went back to Tommie's shop, where she fixed them both a tonic for dyspepsia.

Chapter Twenty-Five

HENRY ERVING was glad to see Finbar arrive at the UPS Store. Even though his new girlfriend had just died, he seemed less upset than when Coral died, but perhaps he was still in shock. In light of the conversation with Don and his sisters, Finbar had a clear line of questioning he wished to pursue with Henry.

"Where's your sidekick?" Henry asked.

"You mean Ms. Watson? She is at her shop cleaning away. They released it as a crime scene. How are you holding up, lad?" Holmes asked.

"All right. At least I didn't touch the poisoned coffee this time, but I hate that I made her drink it. I had no way of knowing it had been poisoned."

"D'you feel you forced her to drink it?"

"Forced is a mighty strong term. I encouraged her. I thought, somehow, we could create a kind of bond … have a place we could enjoy each other's company. I was trying to find some common ground to build a relationship on. I'm 61 years old, and my prospects are dwindling. Bev was younger and so pretty, and for some reason, she wanted to be with me. Go figure. I thought maybe I could build a life with her." He sighed sadly.

"No, I don't believe you forced her, lad. Yer instincts were honorable. Unfortunately, there is a devious killer about. Why would someone wish to harm a lovely lady like Miss Cantrell, d'you think?"

"I have no idea. She really was a wonderful woman. Kind, attentive, attractive. In truth, everything Coral was not."

"Ah, sure, lad. Who's to say who and how we love, eh?"

"That's a good way to put it."

"Henry, d'you like Ms. Watson?"

"Um, you mean like her as a person or as someone to date?"

"No, no. As a person."

"I do like her. She's always been kind to me; she's not judgmental. Coral told me many times how glad she was to have a friend like Ms. Watson. She was especially nice to her."

"What about Mrs. Brewster?"

"Oh, she's the best. And so competent. There could be 20 people in there calling out orders, and she'd never miss a single one. I like both those ladies."

His glowing compliments struck Finbar as

sincere. He could not imagine Henry Erving as a killer or a conspirator, and it made him feel like the man could become a good friend.

"What brings you over here today, Finbar? Do you have something to ship?"

"No, lad. I come to check on you. And I brought you some lovely Guinness in the can. Comes from Ireland, you know."

"Oh, yes, I do. It's a favorite drink of mine, but not many people around here like it because it's strong. How did you know?"

"How could it not be yer favorite, Henry? Yer surname comes from the Gaelic *O hEireamhóin,* does it not? The very root of the name of Ireland. How could you not love Guinness?"

"Does it? How exciting to know that! Thank you, Finbar. I appreciate your consideration."

"Think nothing of it, Henry. I was going to give a pint to Charlie-boy next door, but I've changed my mind. He's a foul-tempered git, isn't he, and I don't like what I hear of how he treated both of yer lady friends."

"He was awful to Coral, that's for sure," Henry agreed, "and to Beverly, too."

"What was his problem, d'you think? Was it because his packages turned up damaged sometimes? That happens with all parcel couriers."

"That's true, especially when they come from someplace like Mexico."

"Mexico, you say? What d'you suppose Mr. Charlie Williams is getting from Mexico?"

Henry looked around to be sure they were alone and then leaned in conspiratorially. "He's getting drugs from there, every week. I'm sure of it."

"You don't say. How can you be sure?"

"Once, when one of his packages came in, Coral was trying to explain to him that it was damaged in transit. He shouted at her and accused her of opening it. She had patched it up the best she could, but he kept hammering at her. She followed him all the way back to his office cussing back at him. That Coral was a feisty one," he laughed.

"Did she see what was in the package?"

"She told me it was full of pills in quart-sized plastic bags. All different kinds of pills. One bag fell out when he snatched the box away from her. We found it on the floor after he left, and Coral kept it stashed in her locker. After she died, I gave it to Beverly to hide for leverage in case Charles tried to push her around and because I had to empty Coral's locker."

"Henry, did Charlie know Beverly had the bag of pills? Did Beverly tell him?"

"I don't think so, Finbar. I told Don, but he wouldn't tell anybody. As far as I know, it's still locked in the bottom drawer of her desk. Do you think it's important? Should I tell Earl Petry?"

"I think you should, lad. It may well be what

caused her death if Charles found out about it. D'you have Officer Petry's number? I think you should go ahead and ring him right now. I'm going back over to Ms. Watson's shop. You enjoy the Guinness, lad. I'll come 'round and pick up the tote some other time. *Sláinte!* That means "health" in Gaelic."

"*Sláinte*," Henry said, "and good health to you, too, Finbar."

Finbar slowly crossed Bottlebrush Boulevard and entered Watson's. Tommie was sitting on her stool measuring herbs on her spotlessly clean counter and filling her dark amber tea canisters with brand new herbal tea blends.

"Haloo, missus. You've done wonders in here," he said. "It looks nearly ready for business."

"Not just yet. I have to replenish a lot of my stock and make several more potions to replace the ones that were ruined, but it's coming along, thanks to you doing the floors and the bathroom. How were your conversations with Henry and Charles?" Tommie was acting more like her usual self.

"I didn't go to see Charlie-boy. Why spoil such a lovely day. I did have a nice chat with Henry. The lad's right broken up about Beverly. I believe he genuinely cared for her, once he got the notion of Coral Beadwell out of his head."

"Do you think Henry should still be a suspect?" she asked.

Finbar took a seat at one of the tables with his back to the door. "I am inclined to remove him, Thomasina. Even though he had ties with both women, his motives don't add up. I would say they are circumstantial at best."

"Why'd he force the coffee on Bev?"

"He was trying to forge a common interest, in his own bumbling way. I truly believe he's harmless, just like Don said."

"But the sisters made those strange faces," she pointed out.

"We must take what they say in tiny spoons, Thomasina. Gossips have a tendency to embellish. I believe it could be they fancy him themselves. But what they said about the drugs, Henry confirmed. Charlie is receiving packages regularly from Mexico. In fact, Coral had a bag of pills from one of Charlie's damaged packages in her locker, and then Henry gave it to Beverly Cantrell earlier this week to lock in her desk drawer."

Tommie almost dropped her knife. "Are you kidding me? Just like Don told us. Beverly had a bag of bootleg pills! Did Charles know?"

"That's unsure. I'm sure Don didn't let it slip to him, but I` told Henry to call the police just before I left his store. He should be doing that now."

She looked up through the window and froze. "He's not calling the police, Finbar. He's going inside the real estate office right this minute. Oh my gosh. Charles will kill him!"

Tommie grabbed her cell phone and dialed Earl's number. Earl answered on the second ring.

"Hello, Tommie," he said smoothly.

"Earl, you need to get to Floral Real Estate right now. Henry Erving's going in there to confront Charles Williams. Hurry, Earl," she begged. "Don't let Charles hurt him."

"Where are you, Tommie?"

"In my shop, looking out the window. I'm safe. You better go quick." She hung up the phone as Finbar disappeared out the front door. She tried to call him back, but it was too late; he was already crossing the street. All she could do was shamble to the door and watch.

In less than two minutes, a police car appeared on Lantana Lane, and Earl Petry emerged from the driver's seat. Tommy watched helplessly as he entered the building. The wait was agonizing, not knowing what was happening or to whom. Suddenly, she saw Earl come through the door holding Henry under the arms, walking him out. She could tell Henry had been beaten; his nose was bleeding. *Where are you, Finbar?* she wondered. *Come out of there, Finbar!*

Earl sat Henry on the sidewalk, and then he grabbed the walkie on his uniform shirt and spoke animatedly into it. He was gesturing at the Silver Linings building. Tommie pressed against the door and craned her neck, trying to see around the gazebo and the oak tree that blocked her line of sight. Earl settled Henry into the passenger seat of his car and then drove off, making a right turn onto Oleander. Finbar had yet to emerge.

Tommie was so focused on looking out the window she failed to hear the back door open. By the time the prickled hairs on her neck alerted her to someone's presence, it was too late. There was a loud thud and an intense pain in her head, and she collapsed to the floor.

The next thing Tommie knew, she was lying on her back, a cold cloth on the base of her skull, and one across her forehead. She heard the faraway sound of someone calling her name, and then she blacked out again.

She awoke in a bed at the Floribunda Urgent Care facility. A white bandage was around her throbbing head and partially obscured her vision. Her mouth was dry as paper.

"Water," she whispered.

A plastic bendy straw was put to her lips, and she sucked it greedily, getting just a little water before it was pulled away.

"That's enough, Thomasina. Just a sip is all."

It's Finbar. Nobody else calls me Thomasina. "What? Who?" she managed aloud.

"Shhh. No talking. You've been bashed on the head rather badly. I found you on yer floor by the front door. Somebody meant to do you harm but must've seen me sprinting across the street. I didn't see who it was. D'you know who hit you?"

She started to shake her head, but the movement caused pain and made tiny flashes of light appear behind her eyes. "No," she croaked.

"I was worried about you, missus."

"Henry?"

"Banged up but recovering. Yer man got there just in time to keep Charlie from beating him to death."

"My man?" She smiled just a little. She didn't say "not my man" this time.

"Charles?"

"Slipped off when we came in. I tried to give chase, but my bad knee won't let me run very well."

"Drugs?"

"Charlie had already found them. He had broken into Beverly's desk drawer. Henry caught him in the act. In the struggle, the bag broke, and pills spilled everywhere. Charlie ran away out the back of his office."

"Got him," she said with the tiniest trace of a smile and a chuckle.

"Not yet. He's still hiding somewhere after coming in yer shop to kill you. I'm so glad I got there in time to scare him off, although who would ever be scared of a 1.70-meter man weighing 10 stone, I don't know."

"Stupid metric system," she whispered before closing her aching eyes.

When she next opened them, the man holding her hand was not Finbar; it was Earl Petry.

"I kept my promise, Earl. I didn't investigate,"

she said.

"I know. Mr. Holmes told me. And you still got hurt. Lord, but you're a stubborn woman, Tommie Watson," he said gruffly, but Tommie could hear the softness underneath.

"Charles?"

"We caught him not far from here. He's locked up. We found all sorts of illegal prescription drugs from Mexico in his office and at his house. He won't be walking around for a good while."

"Linda?"

"We'll interrogate her to see how much she knew. It could be jail for Mrs. Linda Beadwell if she was in cahoots with him."

"Henry?"

"Doing fine. He finally stood up to someone."

"Earl?"

"Right where he needs to be."

"Thanks for sharing," she said.

"Thanks for living," he replied.

Chapter Twenty-Six

TOMMIE WATSON spent the rest of that night on Camelia Street—sleeping in Finbar's guest bedroom. Because she had a concussion, he was vigilant, staying up all night to watch her. He gently roused her every hour, asking if she knew her name and where she was. After the sixth time, she told him she was the Queen of Hearts and she was going to cut off his head if he didn't stop. He laughed and told her she was mad. She told him he didn't know the half of it.

She slept off and on throughout the night and part of the next day. Finbar darkened the room and regularly applied a cool, moist cloth to the place where she had been struck. He kept the dogs quiet, letting them romp around outside as long as they wanted. Earl called several times and talked to Holmes, who assured him Tommie was being well looked after.

By Saturday afternoon, Tommie was ready to

leave the guest room. Finbar helped her onto the sofa and brought her a cup of the herbal tea blend she had made him with plenty of her *Honey-Honey*. He gently massaged her neck and shoulders and found a station on the cable television network that played her favorite soothing new age music.

That night, whether it was the tea, the head injury, or the constant care, she slept soundly. When she woke the next day, she was starving.

"Would you like a toast and butter with marmalade, missus?" Finbar asked.

"Yes, I'd love that for starters, but then I want some real food," she answered.

Finbar laughed. "And what would her Majesty desire for breakfast?"

"Fried spuds and black pudding."

"I think yer head was harder than the thing what hit it, Thomasina. But sure, if that's what you want, that's what we'll eat. Drink yer tea, lass, and have yer toast. Breakfast'll be ready in just a minute."

He brought her a tray and insisted she stay on the sofa. When she argued that she was a messy eater, he laid a dish towel over her chest. He took his on a tray at his easy chair, and the two of them ate silently, savoring the food and the quiet comfort of their growing friendship. When they finished, the dogs got the scraps and he put the plates in to soak.

"Finbar, did they figure out what was used to

club me?" she asked.

"They did, lad It was yer marble grinder from yer counter. It made a right bloody dent in yer hard head."

"Well, crap. I had just cleaned it, too."

"Thomasina, it's lucky it wasn't delivered with more force. It could've crushed yer skull. Had Charlie not seen me coming, he might've hit you a lot more. Bloody rotter. Glad he's been caught."

"But you were there, and he's been stopped, and that's that."

Tommie shifted positions. The movement made her feel dizzy and a little sick to her stomach. Finbar saw her eyes roll, and her face became pale.

"Thomasina, you need to stay here a few more days. Myself and Sherlock love yer company and yer dogs, too. It's no bother."

Tommie protested, at first, but he told her he felt it was his responsibility to watch over her in case her head injury proved to be more serious than what the doctors said. Tommie knew it wasn't about the head injury; he secretly felt guilty for leaving her alone that day. She could see it in the way he looked at her from the corner of his eye and his constant attention to her needs.

Although Monday was President's Day, and Tommie had some great ideas for President-themed tea blends, Finbar and Earl both encouraged her to wait, so she decided to rest for another week at Finbar's and a week at her own unit before she tried reopening her shop.

Besides, her head was still so tender that she was unable to lie on her back, and the constant swapping from side to side made her irritable. She didn't want to inflict that frame of mind on her customers.

Finbar didn't take drop-ins at his home, but he was more than willing to let people bring cards and food baskets to the door for Tommie. She had a few phone calls from Don Lareby and the sisters to check on her, and Sarah Beth had called several times and dropped off a big basket of cheese, crackers, and chocolates. She even got a picnic hamper of baked goods from the Trinity LCO and a sweet card. Henry visited Finbar one evening, and the two of them played poker and drank Guinness while Tommie napped on the sofa.

The week after her attack, when Tommie was ready to go back to her side of the duplex, Finbar asked her to stay two more days at his place. She was still suffering from headaches and double vision. Not having the strength or the inclination to refuse, she stayed. He told her that he would have her duplex unit cleaned and spiffed up for her return, and that was fine with Tommie.

On Wednesday the 20th, Tommie felt like she had imposed long enough. She was ready to go home. Finbar walked her over to the kitchen door and held it open for her. One step inside, and she almost lost consciousness again.

"What have you done?" she asked.

"I told you I would fix up yer home, missus. I

hope you like it," he said, trying to hide a big smile.

Tommie couldn't believe the change. The uneven brown painted concrete floor had been covered with beautiful, grey-toned tongue and groove wood planks that matched the newly painted dove-grey walls. The ugly outdated ceiling tiles were covered with smooth white plaster, and the lighting throughout the space consisted of industrial wood and metal fixtures, reflecting Tommie's eclectic style. Each room had a matching ceiling fan, which proved to be both decorative and functional. He had even replaced her lumpy worn living room loveseat with a loveseat and chaise combination set in a gun metal grey nubby fabric similar to his brown sofa. Tommie's favorite improvements, though, were the locking doggie doors out of the kitchen and bedroom into the fenced-in back yard. It was a home that Tommie had dreamed of, so much like her cottage in the woods that it made her heart ache.

"How did you know what I'd like?" she asked.

"I know you, missus," he said, "and you have scores of pictures of yer cottage on yer phone. I couldn't help but look at them while you slept. And before you wonder, I've moved yer herbs and potion making things to the little shed under the carpark, and I put in metal shelves and an air conditioner to keep them cool and dry. Welcome home, Thomasina Watson. Welcome home, Zed and Red."

Tommie threw her arms around his neck and

cried, and Finbar cried a little, too. When she pulled back, he gave her one more surprise. It was an envelope with her name printed on the front in his tidy handwriting.

"What's this?" she asked.

"Well, seeing as I'm yer landlord, I wanted to give you a new arrangement with my rental terms. All you need to do is sign it, if you please, just at the bottom."

Tommie opened it with trembling fingers. It was a simple document of only a few lines of writing and a signature line. It read: *Tenancy Agreement between Thomasina Watson and Finbar Holmes. On this 20ᵗʰ day of February 2019, Unit A of the duplex at 3095 Camelia Street, Floribunda, Florida, owned by Mr. Finbar Holmes, is hereby leased indefinitely to Ms. Thomasina Watson for an open-ended period of time at a fixed rental price of $10 per month.*

Chapter Twenty-Seven

FRIDAY, MARCH 1, 2019 was the grand re-opening of Watson's Reme-Teas. Tommie could hardly believe the crowd of people standing outside waiting for her to let them in. So much had happened in the month since she received that disappointing phone call from Beverly Cantrell that it was hard to keep it all straight.

Charles Williams had been indicted for buying and distributing the illegal drugs from Mexico. He was set to be tried the following month and faced the maximum sentence allowed by the State of Florida. He confessed to the drug deals but refused to admit to the murders of Coral Beadwell and Beverly Cantrell. In fact, he adamantly denied having any involvement in their deaths. As the evidence against him was largely circumstantial, and without a confession of guilt, the indictment on those charges was pending a more extensive investigation. He also denied the assault and battery charges related to his fight with Henry Erving, as well as the attack on Tommie Watson.

Linda Beadwell was not found to be complicit in the conspiracy to distribute illegal drugs. She claimed she knew nothing about Charles Williams' side business. The affair did come to light, however, and Thomas Beadwell promptly filed for divorce. He arranged to buy the Beadwell House, but his intention was for it to be turned into an historical museum of the Beadwell founding family. The commission for the sale was given to the now renamed Floribunda Real Property Company. Its new owners were a brother and two sisters: Don Lareby, Susan Clay, and Elaine Frank.

Tommie had a talk with the Reverend Gerald Lamb of Trinity Episcopal Church. He wisely counseled the Trinity Ladies' Charity Organization to alternate their monthly meetings between Brewster's Coffee Shoppe and Watson's Reme-Teas.

Tommie had not been well enough to attend the funeral of Coral Beadwell or the memorial observance for Beverly Cantrell. Finbar went and represented her at each woman's service.

Earl had phoned her several nights and even dropped by the house one afternoon during his shift. Tommie could tell she was still a "person of interest," but Earl was known for taking his time about romances. She was perfectly fine with taking it slowly … at least, for the time being.

Afraid that Charles had planted any more poison after he knocked Tommy unconscious, Earl had the crime scene technicians test small samples of all her exposed herbs and blends for contaminants. Finbar and Henry went one evening and recleaned every surface with alcohol and peroxide. They washed all the cups and knives and sanitized them in the dishwasher (which Finbar had replaced with a new model) to be certain they were safe for use.

The morning of the grand opening, Sanderson Harper called Tommie on the phone.

"Hey, Tommie. It's Sandy. I've got some news for you regarding the causes of death for Coral and Beverly which we've just finished up."

"Was it cyanide poisoning?" Tommie asked.

"It was poisoning, but not exactly cyanide, although it presented like cyanide," he drawled.

"What are you saying, Sandy?"

"Both Coral Beadwell and Beverly Cantrell died of *torsades de pointes.*"

"Which is what?"

"It's an abnormal heart arrythmia which leads to instantaneous cardiac death."

"Heart attack?" She was surprised.

"Not in the sense that one usually has a heart attack. The cardiac events were brought on due to the introduction of poisons into their systems."

"Did you just say poisons—as in plural? More

than one poison?" she asked.

"Yes, I did. Plural. Both women ingested the same combination of ingredients in considerable doses, but they metabolized them differently because of their underlying conditions and the medications each of them was taking. Do I need to dumb it down for you to make it easier to understand?"

"Nope. I understand perfectly. Remember, I told you before that I had to take extensive training, which included learning medical jargon, physiology, and the specific herbal contraindications with traditional medications, so go on."

"Super. Love being able to talk shop with someone who actually knows what I'm saying. The official toxicology findings confirm that the poisons were a lethal combination of prescription medications— specifically fluoxetine, citalopram, haloperidol, and cimetidine. Those are the active ingredients in the non-generic meds known as Prozac, Celexa, Haldol, and Tagamet. They are normally legitimately prescribed separately for a number of illnesses or conditions."

"Hang on, let me write this down. OK. Go on."

"Fluoxetine is an anti-depressant that is also taken for obsessive compulsive disorder. Citalopram is a serotonin reuptake inhibitor, or SSRI, as well. It is commonly used for depression. Haloperidol is an antipsychotic prescribed for bipolar disorder, and cimetidine is a common over-the-counter drug taken for acid reflux. When combined and ingested in large doses, they mimic the symptoms of cyanide poisoning. In fact, Celexa and Tagamet actually contain trace amounts of sodium cyanide, potassium cyanide, hydrogen cyanide, and cyangen cyanide."

"I've got you, so far. That's very interesting. You said something about interacting with medications each victim was taking? Can you elaborate on that?

"Yup. Coral Beadwell had been taking Biaxin for strep throat. Biaxin is a mycin drug, specifically clarithromycin. On top of that, her stomach contents reveal she had drunk grapefruit juice that morning, which decreases the activity of the enzymes that break down drugs and toxins. In combination with the already toxic drug cocktail, the onset of *torsades de pointes* in Coral occurred quickly."

"I thought Coral looked like she was having a heart attack," Tommie commented.

"She absolutely was. Good observation, cousin. Let me get to the next woman. All right, here we go. Beverly Cantrell had been prescribed levofloxacin, known commonly as Levaquin. It's used as an antibiotic for sinusitis and urinary tract infections. Beverly had both. She had also been taking phentermine—an amphetamine used for weight loss—for a long period of time. That, plus the other drugs on an empty stomach and the addition of caffeine into her system caused her fatal cardiac event. She was dead when she hit the floor."

"Wow. What accounted for their red faces?"

"The cyanides in the drugs plus the elevated blood pressure caused the flushing. Another good catch on your part, Tommie."

"And are these drugs that are easily acquired?"

"With the exception of the Tagamet, you need a prescription from a doctor for them."

"Did you find them in the pills Charles Williams got from Mexico?"

"Yup. All but the Tagamet and the Levaquin. He had quite the cornucopia in his possession. And to think, I went to church with that man ... and he was a Deacon, too. Oversaw the finances and organized the budget, of all things! You never know, right?" Sandy said.

"Nope. You never do. Thanks, Sandy. That clears up a lot for me. The fruit pits, rocks, and kernels were not really an issue, huh?"

"Gotta cover all the bases. But it's good information for you to keep in your back pocket, just in case. Right?"

"Right. Thanks again, Sandy. Oh, hey! Are you coming to my reopening this afternoon?" she asked.

"I will absolutely be there. I love what you've done with the shop. It almost makes me want to be a tea drinker ... well, not really, but I do like your changes. See you," he said.

Tommie hung up and checked her watch. Seeing it was already 9:30, she hurried to finish getting ready.

She divided a can of Vienna Sausages for the dogs and checked her makeup and hair for the 10th time. Although it was a special occasion, she decided to stick with her usual work outfit of loose-fitting scrubs. The set she wore today was dark teal. They were freshly pressed, and the pants leg was wide enough to fit over the walking boot, making it less conspicuous. Thankfully, in another 2 ½ weeks she would finally be able to go without it.

Tommie grabbed her cane and traipsed happily out the front door. As she approached the carport, she saw Finbar waiting beside the car, holding her door open. He was dressed in khaki slacks and a green plaid button-down collar shirt. A traditional Trinity tweed flat cap of tan Herringbone was perched on his head, making him the picture of an Irish gentleman.

"How handsome you look, Finbar," she remarked, sliding into the driver's seat.

"Thank you, missus. It's a special occasion, so I thought I'd dress the part. Yer new outfit is quite stunning," he quipped with a grin.

They drove the few blocks into town and parked at the back of the shop. As soon as they entered, Sarah Beth appeared through the connecting door. She gave Tommie a big hug and greeted Finbar.

"I am so glad to see you, Tommie. It hasn't been the same without you on the other side. You look good. How's the head?" she intoned.

"Much better, Sarah Beth. Thank you for the box

of chocolates, by the way. They worked better than anything else."

"Don't they always?" Sarah Beth laughed and pulled the door between the shops closed.

"Do you not have any customers, lad?" Finbar asked Sarah Beth.

"Not anymore. I closed up at 9:00 so I could be here to help Tommie with her reopening."

"You are the best, Sarah Beth," Tommie said.

"Ah, go on. How can you use me?"

"Well, if you'd unpack those treats and set them out to look pretty on the marble top, that'd be a big help. The plexiglass sneeze guard over the counter will keep them from getting contaminated."

"So, you're setting them up buffet style and giving them away for free?"

"Yeah. People can grab a disposable plate and help themselves. We can let them line up at the end over there, and then make their way to the front counter to get their tea."

"Oh, wow. These look delicious. What are they? And can I have one of each now?" Sarah Beth asked.

"Go ahead and grab some. I've got *Late-for-a-Date Tea Biscuits, Mad Hatter Muffins, March Hare Madeleines,* and *Dormouse Delights.*"

"You come up with the most creative names. They're perfect for your 'Out of the Rabbit Hole' theme. When did you make all these?"

"I didn't. Finbar did. He's quite the culinary wizard in the kitchen!"

"It's just a hobby of mine. But sure, the missus needed to focus on other matters, so I baked," he said.

"You're a prize, Mr. Holmes. Wish I had you at my house and in my shop. Oh, that reminds me. My son Barry is coming by to help us out, if that's OK. I'll put him down here to show people where to start the line."

"Aw, that's great, Sarah Beth. Barry was a big help getting me ready for my first opening. He reminds me of my own son Kevin. They're both good fellows."

"Thanks. No problem. While I'm nibbling, I'll set up your treats. Do you want the 'Eat Me' sign to go on the counter or the sneeze guard?"

"Set it on the counter, please, and the 'Drink Me' sign goes here at the pick-up counter. I made up those little 3x5 placards for each treat with the name and a picture of the *Alice in Wonderland* character. They're small, so you can stick them just above the edge of the sneeze guard with tape over each plate of treats once you've arranged them."

"What order do you want them?"

"I don't care. Arrange them anyway you'd like. I trust your judgment. You're very organized and orderly that way. You truly have a gift, Sarah Beth."

"Yeah, sometimes my OCD comes in handy. What kinds of special tea blends are you serving?"

"I've got *Teadle-Dee* and *Teadle-Dum.* The first

one is a mix of blackberry leaf, peppermint, lemon balm, lavender flowers, and marshmallow leaf, and the second one is made with red clover herb and blossoms, spearmint, lemon peel, and thyme. *Queen of Hearts* is a flowering tea with red rose petals, raspberry leaf, and jasmine blossoms tied with green tea leaves. And I made one especially for you and your coffee drinkers with roasted chicory, mocha mix, roasted dandelion root, and roasted carob. It's called *Cheshire Cat Coffee.*" Tommie winked at her. "You can serve it in your shop, too."

Sarah Beth teared up and raced for the restroom.

"What did I say wrong?" Tommie asked in alarm as Sarah Beth disappeared.

"I don't know that you said anything wrong, missus. I think she was touched that you've included her, especially with the addition of the coffee-flavored blend. Just let her get on with it. She'll be to rights shortly," Finbar answered.

About the time Sarah Beth came out of the bathroom, Barry Brewster entered. He seemed like a hazy shadow in comparison to his mother. She showed him where to stand and told him what to say. All the while, he nodded slowly, barely showing any emotion. Tommie unintentionally scrutinized him. *That poor boy takes medication for depression, but I don't think it's doing him any good,* she thought.

Tommie caught his eye and waved, and Barry gave the slightest trace of a smile and waved back. To her surprise, he walked toward her and held out a small white box with gold writing which read *Bettina's Baubles*.

"What's this, Barry?" Tommie cocked her head as she held the box.

"Mom and I got this from the jewelry store for your reopening. I picked it out." He blinked rapidly, avoiding eye contact.

Tommie removed the lid of the box. Inside was a silver filigree stickpin with a colorful enameled teacup and saucer on the top.

"Barry! It's perfect!" she cried, gathering the slight young man in an embrace. He stood woodenly at first, but Tommie felt his slender arms reach around and pat her back exactly twice before he broke away and returned to his mother.

"Am I too early?" Earl said from the back door.

Tommie whirled toward the voice and nearly lost her balance. She gave him her brightest smile and motioned him inside.

"Never too early, Earl. I'm glad you're here," she said as she pinned the teacup to her shoulder.

Earl ambled in and spoke to Sarah Beth, shook the listless Barry's hand, and sidled up to Holmes.

"Finbar. Thanks for taking care of our girl. She looks good ... and rested, for a change," he said.

"I'm afraid it's going to be my calling in life, looking after our Ms. Watson," Finbar said with a laugh.

"I'll be happy to spell you for a bit anytime. Just

give me a call. She's a hard one to keep out of trouble."

"That she is. That she is."

"I'm right here, guys," Tommie said, raising her voice up a notch. "I hear you talking."

The two men exchanged a knowing look.

"She hears us talking," Finbar commented.

"Yeah, she's right there," Earl agreed.

"Thomasina, it's almost on the hour," Finbar said, glancing at the clock.

"Dangit. I lost track of the time," she lamented.

"I find that hard to believe." Earl glanced at the huge clock on her wall.

Tommie let out a *hmph* and took a last look around the shop. Everything seemed to be in place. The window displays were bright and colorful representations of the tea party from the *Alice in Wonderland* children's novel. Cloth covered tables in each window were topped with teapots of various colors, shapes, and materials from her own home, as well as mismatched teacups and saucers filled with fresh flowers. Flea market cups were stacked precariously and glued in place, and plates were piled with imitation sandwiches. Here and there, she had situated stuffed characters from the story: Mad Hatter, Cheshire Cat, Dormouse in a pot, and a white rabbit in a waistcoat with a gigantic pocket watch. While the line formed outside, she could see the people pointing to the different elements in the display. It was organized chaos, and it completely reflected her personality. Tommie's approach to decorating was at the complete other end of the spectrum from Sarah Beth's meticulously ordered and regimented style. *It must be from her OCD,* she thought.

"Time, missus!" Finbar called.

Tommie made her way to the door and turned the sign from CLOSED to OPEN. The group outside cheered. She swung the door wide and welcomed each and every one of them individually as they filed in. Soon, the shop was filled with customers and friends who mingled with one another and exclaimed over the decorations and the treats. Tommie sat on her stool (which made her a much-needed couple of inches taller) and clapped her hands. The guests shushed each other and turned toward her quietly.

"My friends. You have made me so welcome here in Floribunda. I never knew I could grow to love a place so much in such a short time. It's been a very tough and trying few weeks, but today, I am out of the rabbit hole!"

The crowd clapped and cheered. She signaled for quiet again. "Today I want to show my appreciation to you. You've saved my life and made me your friend. I especially want to mention some of the folks who have really come through for me: my Irish friend and neighbor Finbar Holmes, my shop buddy Sarah Beth Brewster, my valuable helper Barry Brewster, my cousin Sanderson Harper, my friends Maggie and Craig Kohl, Annie Lang, Terry Jackson, Henry Erving, Don Lareby, Susan Clay, Elaine Frank, and Floribunda's finest policeman Earl

Petry. Please, help yourself to some tea party treats and a cup of herbal tea blend."

Having made her speech, and to another round of applause, Tommie got down from her stool and began making tea for her guests. As she prepared their orders, she sipped a bottled water and nibbled from a plate of treats Earl had set to the side for her. Barry Brewster directed the people through the food line competently, and Tommie even saw him begin smiling and having conversations. She nodded and winked at Barry in appreciation as she patted the pin on her shoulder. She him a big 'thumbs-up' sign, and she was almost certain the young man blushed.

Sarah Beth came behind the counter and helped out by pouring water into the teacups after Tommie filled the tea ball infusers with the desired blends. She kept the kettles filled and served the steaming teas on ceramic saucers. When the self-service items got low, she watched proudly as Barry hustled to replenish them.

Finbar and Henry circulated among the guests and kept up lively conversations, clearing off the tables and taking the trash out to the dumpster in back. Tommie was amazed at the difference in Henry Erving. Formerly dour and unsure of himself, he had the sisters in stitches. It was comical to watch them each vying for his attention.

Earl made polite small talk with people in the room, but he stuck pretty close to Tommie, taking up a place just on the other side of the cash register in front of the coolers.

Tommie was glad for the extra help and especially for Earl's presence and attention. She wondered idly if anything more would come from their friendship. *Nope. Don't even go there, Tommie,* she told herself. *Let whatever comes happen in its own time, just like this blooming tea blend.*

When things began to settle down, and everyone was relaxing at the tables and along the walls, Finbar walked to the counter and had Tommie refill his cup. "Fix yerself a cup, too, missus. It's time for me to give a toast," he whispered.

Tommie grabbed her jumbo Zed and Red cup and filled it with boiling water, immersed a tea ball stuffed with a bit of both *Teadle* blends into it, and added honey from a squeeze bottle beneath the counter. She topped it with a splash of bottled water to cool it down and held the teacup in her hand as Finbar turned and faced the crowd.

"I've come to know Missus Thomasina in just a month's time, and I believe she is one of the finest lassies I've ever known. So, I'd like to propose a toast. Raise yer cups, lads, to Thomasina Watson." He held his cup aloft.

"To Thomasina Watson," the guests repeated.

Tommie raised her cup and brought it to her lips. Things happened quickly from that point on, but to Tommie, the events were in slow motion.

"No! Oh, dear God! No! Tommie, don't drink

it!" Sarah Beth screamed.

From the corner of her eye, Tommie saw Sarah Beth leap toward her. She knocked the cup from Tommie's hand, and it smashed on the floor at the foot of her stool. Earl Petry grabbed Tommie by the shoulders and literally lifted her over the counter. Finbar turned and blocked the walk through, preventing Sarah Beth from leaving. Barry shouted for his mother, who had crumpled to the floor in tears. The sisters screamed and rushed into Henry's arms. Don stood up and actually called 9-1-1 this time. Maggie, Craig, Terry, and Annie huddled together against the front door. Sandy pushed in behind the counter and guarded the spilled tea and broken teacup. Tommie hid her face in Earl's chest and sobbed.

Chapter Twenty-Eight

TOMMIE AND FINBAR settled themselves in Tommie's house. He sat on the loveseat with his feet up on the square ottoman, and she reclined on the chaise with her legs outstretched. The three dogs were sprawled on the area rug on the floor.

"D'you know that yer an exhausting woman to be around, Thomasina?" Finbar said, taking a swallow from his second cold can of Guinness.

"You think it's exhausting for you? You should be in my position!" she said, noisily slurping from her second cup of *Zzzzz-Tea.*

Finbar sighed and shook his head. "I missed it. I completely missed it," he said with a groan.

"You only missed it because I hadn't yet shared with you what Sandy told me on the phone. You'd have put it together immediately."

"Did you?" he asked.

"Not until it was almost too late. I had one of those uncomfortable feelings, like when you know something, but you just can't put your finger on it."

"What made you discomforted?"

"Something Sarah Beth said about arranging the snacks. She said that her OCD came in handy sometimes. It made me think of our conversation with the siblings. Elaine said that Prozac was an adult medication for OCD."

"They also told us that Gary Brewster takes a medication for bipolar disorder, and the son takes Celexa for his depression."

"Yes, that didn't register until I saw Barry talking with his mother. I remember thinking to myself that his depression medication wasn't working. That should've been a dead giveaway, but it went right over my head."

"Celexa is citalopram. That's one of the medications I read about on the internet. I'm such an idjit. It should've registered."

"Too late to beat ourselves up about it now."

"But, we might've lost you, lad. How could I have lived with that? D'you know how important you are to me, Thomasina Watson?"

"About as much as you are to me, and our dogs to each other. I wish Earl would call. I'm anxious to hear what Sarah Beth had to say. I still can't believe she actually killed Coral and Beverly."

"She nearly killed you twice, Thomasina. I

misjudged that one all right. Idjit!" he said, draining his can of ale.

Earl didn't call; he came over. Tommie welcomed him in. Once the dogs settled down, Finbar gave up his seat on the loveseat to Earl and sat in the grey leatherette armchair in the corner across from them, his bare feet on the small round matching ottoman.

Tommie cocked her head and smiled at Earl.

"Would you like a cup of tea?" she asked.

"No, thank you, Tommie. I'd rather have what Finbar's having."

Finbar hopped up and went to the refrigerator. He came back with two more cold cans of Guinness.

"Sláinte! That means 'health' in Gaelic," he said, handing Earl the can.

"Same to you," Earl replied, raising the can. The act of toasting made him wince as he remembered how close Tommie had come to being poisoned. He glanced at her quickly, and then he upended the can and drank down nearly half of the cold ale.

Finbar and Tommie stared at him. Neither of them spoke.

Earl wiped his mouth and burped silently with his mouth closed, and then he drained the can.

"Dangit, boy," Tommie said, barely restraining a guffaw. "Finbar, I think he needs another."

She needn't have said anything; he was already on his way back from the refrigerator with a fresh cold one.

Earl accepted the can, but he drank this one slowly, savoring the cold bitterness on his tongue as he tried to choose his words. Finbar and Tommie waited patiently for him to speak.

"Sarah Beth confessed to the poisonings, and to clocking you on the head, Tommie."

"Why, Earl? For the life of me, I can't understand it," she said, shaking her head slowly.

"Not really supposed to tell you, this having yet to go through the legal process, but if I don't, you two will do your own dadblamed investigating. Am I right?"

Tommie and Finbar shrugged innocently.

"Aw hell. Sarah Beth has more of a buttoned-up life that you'd think. She and Gary and their son are all on medication. To the outside world, they seem happy and well adjusted, but they're really pretty dysfunctional. That son of theirs is clinical and should probably be institutionalized. He's attempted suicide more than once. Gary's bipolar, and unless he's on his meds, he's liable to be either manic depressive or hyped up higher than a monkey eating coffee beans."

It wasn't funny, but Tommie had to put her teacup to her mouth to keep from laughing. *Stress or shock. Just hold it together,* she told herself. Thankfully, Earl didn't notice.

"Between the two of them, Sarah Beth walked a tightrope, never knowing when Barry might attempt suicide or when Gary will snap and be abusive. I've known them all my life, but I honestly never expected anything like this from Sarah Beth. OCD isn't something that makes you try to kill people."

"Then why did she?" Tommie asked, her voice soft and low.

"She was jealous; she was ambitious. Maybe she was desperate. When Sandy got tired of his pitiful excuse for a sandwich shop, she had visions of renting both shops and making one big business."

"My gosh. Just like Charles," Tommie said.

"Pretty much. That's one reason she hated him. He had the means to buy both shops, and she didn't."

"But, Earl. I told her they're Harper properties. Sandy can't sell them outside the family. She could never have bought them. Neither could Charles."

"You know that, but Sarah Beth didn't. She thought you were a renter, just like her. Then, when you told her Sandy wouldn't sell, she just figured she could coerce him somehow into giving her a long-term lease. Same difference in her eyes."

"But only if you were out of the picture, lad," Finbar said, "one way or another."

"Exactly," Earl said. "Even if she couldn't buy them, she would have a place for Barry to work so she could keep an eye on him, and it would give her a cushion to fall back on in case Gary went completely over the edge one day and either left her or beat her senseless."

"But how was killing Coral Beadwell even an

option for her?" Tommie asked.

"She didn't intend to kill Coral. In fact, she didn't intend to kill anyone."

"Coral wasn't the target; Thomasina was," Finbar stated, "or rather her shop was."

"Bingo! You got it. Sarah Beth used her key and went into your shop that Monday morning aiming to put something into a cup that would make one of your customers sick. The things she had available were medications from her own house: Haldol, Prozac, Celexa, and Tagamet. She crushed up some of the pills and put the powder in a piece of tinfoil. Linda Beadwell was beating on Brewster's door before 6:00 a.m., wanting to get in so she could be there when Charles arrived. Sarah Beth panicked, afraid she'd been seen, and dumped the whole packet of crushed pills into the first cup she came into contact with. It happened to be Coral's. She told me she didn't even know Coral had a favorite cup."

"It could just as easily have been *yers*, missus, just like you said," Finbar noted.

Tommie shivered, and Earl patted her leg. "I don't even want to think about that, but it could have. Back to her confession. Just before you opened, Linda came back into her shop and began to argue with her. Knowing you'd soon have customers, and wanting to be get away before then, she rushed Linda out the back and drove to the *Winn Dixie* where she had the butcher cut up a special order for her, giving herself a solid alibi."

"So, it was to discredit me? To put me out of business so she could take over my shop?" Tommie asked.

"Yes. Charles planted that idea by telling people your cups weren't sanitary and your dishwasher was old. I like the new one, by the way. And Linda fed into it by saying she didn't know what was in your herbal tea blends. Funny how things like that can stick in someone's mind and be twisted."

"That seems so lame, though. Who thinks like that?" Tommie asked.

"Someone desperate, as yer friend must've been," Finbar said.

"Not *my* friend," Tommie huffed.

"Oh, but she was, missus, or else you'd be dead."

"Why would she kill Beverly?" Tommie asked.

"Oh, that was unintentional, too. Beverly was not the target. Charles Williams was," Earl said, taking a hefty swig of his ale.

"What? Charles? Did she intend to make him sick, too? I can't see the purpose in that," Tommie stated.

"No, no, no. She *intended* to *kill* Charles. He stood in the way of her getting her heart's desire—the two shops. You, yourself, told her that Sanderson could never sell, but he could give Charles a long-term lease on both the shops," Earl told her. "I know you didn't mean to, but you put that bug in her head, Tommie."

"I don't know what to say."

"Let me finish, then. Your shop was closed

down, maybe indefinitely. It was Valentine's Day, and you brought her those snacks. In her own twisted way, she truly liked you, and you always came through for her. She didn't even know you'd be there that day, though, and she had already dosed a large mug to give to Charles. You threw a monkey wrench into the works. By trying to help, you only got her more flustered. She had OCD, and everything had to be ordered and done in a particular way. You're so laid back, it made it difficult for her to focus. When it got busy, and you couldn't keep up, she jumped in to fix things. She grabbed the mug she had set aside for Charles and put Beverly's coffee in it by mistake."

"I had no idea. I thought I was helping," she said.

"I know, Darlin'. I know," Earl said, patting her on the hand.

"So, when Beverly died, it served some of the same purpose as Charlie dying would have. It took focus away from Sarah Beth because it looked like she was being targeted, too," Finbar deduced.

"I can't imagine being that messed up," Tommie said, leaning her head back against the chaise. She winced when the bruise on her head came into contact with the cushion. She sat up abruptly.

"What is it, missus?" Finbar asked.

"*She. Hit. Me. On. The. Back. Of. My. Head*," she said through gritted teeth.

"That she did. It was Sarah Beth in yer shop, not Charlie," Finbar said.

"Yep. By then, she was beyond desperate. She had killed once, and after the first time, it gets easier, I'm afraid," Earl said. "You were alone, and it was a perfect opportunity to get rid of you for good. Besides, as clever as you and Holmes were, she knew it was just a matter of time before the two of you figured it out. Both of you had been in there cleaning, so she knew you'd be opening in a day or two. Caving in your skull was not her first option. She wanted to poison you, but you were standing right there when she came in the back door, and you would have seen her any minute. There wouldn't have been a good reason for her to be in your shop. She couldn't have come in through the connecting door because *she* actually listened to me when I said to stay out of the crime scene!" He gave Tommie a stern look.

"Earl, d'you think her OCD condition had anything to do with her attacking Thomasina like she did?" Finbar asked.

"Oh, absolutely. You take a person who's got to be in control of every minute detail, and you move one little thing out of place, and that person will spiral out of control. Y'all didn't move one little thing—y'all moved a lot of little things."

"When did she poison my cup?" Tommie asked.

"Oh, that could've been anytime between the time we caught Charles and released her shop as a crime scene and today before your grand reopening. She had plenty of opportunity to do it," Earl said.

"But after Henry and I cleaned it up. She, of course, knew when we were there. Earl, why d'you think she stopped Thomasina from drinking the poison?" Finbar asked, although he already knew the answer.

Earl turned to Tommie. "She liked you, Tommie. She really did. And today, you were sweet and trusting and appreciative. You accepted her help with such graciousness. You allowed her to make the decision about the snack arrangement and complimented her handicap by calling it a gift. But, more than anything, you were kind to her son. She saw you wave at him and wink at him and smile at him. You hugged him, and she saw him respond to the genuine beauty you have inside. She said he even laughed and interacted with other people because of something you touched in him. She was no longer Sarah Beth, the woman who was in control and wanted to run a large coffee shop. She was Sarah Beth, the mother of a troubled child. You showed them both love, Tommie Watson, and that's what turned Sarah Beth." He had his hand on her shoulder, and he didn't pat it; he just let it lie there, heavy and warm and comforting as the tears rolled down her cheeks.

Finbar finished his Guinness, the dogs snored on the floor, and everything was good in Tommie's world.

Chapter Twenty-Nine

ST. PATRICK'S DAY arrived on a Sunday, and it was a time for celebration. Tommie had been given permission to remove the monstrous black boot, and she made her way around slowly with the help of a bright teal cane Finbar had ordered for her.

"You need something to match yer shop décor, missus," he explained when he presented it.

Sarah Beth pled guilty to the manslaughter of Coral Beadwell and Beverly Cantrell, attempted murder of Charles Williams, and attempted murder of Thomasina Watson. She made a plea deal to serve her sentence in a minimum-security facility where she would receive mental health treatment.

Charles Williams was found guilty of his drug charges, and he was sent to the Floral County Correctional Facility in Cypress City to serve out his lengthy sentence.

Following the divorce, Linda Beadwell moved to Ag City, Alabama and got a job in a retail department store as a salesperson.

Henry Erving began keeping company with both of the sisters. For some unknown reason, it was a satisfactory arrangement for all of them, and the trio was frequently seen eating lunch in the gazebo or at the *Lunch Pad* with Don Lareby.

Gary Brewster did indeed go over the edge after Sarah Beth was arrested. He got in his car one morning, drove away, and never returned to Floribunda.

Barry Brewster checked himself into a recovery center in Sugar Sands Beach where he could be near the beauty of the blue-green gulf water. Tommie and her son Kevin visited him every Sunday after their dinner at Kevin's restaurant. He began teaching Barry to play the guitar, and the young man finally got the positive attention he needed. Maggie promised to light a pink candle for him and send positive thoughts.

Terry Jackson and Annie Lang took Tommie and Finbar to a Mexican restaurant on the outskirts of Floribunda. After he finished wiping down the table and the silverware, Finbar thoroughly enjoyed the food and asked to be invited again. He, of course, paid the check and left a generous tip.

Earl took Tommie to dinner two Saturday nights in a row. The first time was to Sam's Bar-B-Q, a local favorite. The second time was to The Fallen Oak, a restaurant that used to be called The Great Oak before the hurricane. They did not invite Finbar to accompany them; she did not wear scrubs.

Kevin Watson had to work on St. Patrick's Day, so Tommie's evening was freed up to go with Earl to the grand opening of a new establishment in town. The seating was reserved for only 20 guests, and Tommie and Earl had been personally invited by the proud proprietor. They arrived at 4:45 and took their seats. They were pleased to see Henry there with Don and the sisters. Their tables were beside each other.

It was a casual, but exclusive, dining place that served light snacks and beverages for customers to enjoy while they watched a cooking demonstration by the owner. The menu always reflected the latest holiday or celebration. Being St. Patrick's Day, the meal was Irish themed. While they waited, Earl had an Irish coffee and Tommie had Irish tea.

At 5:00, the owner, dressed in chef's clothing of black and white striped pants and a white jacket, donned a tall white starched chef's hat for the cooking exhibition. He proceeded to demonstrate how to make the night's dinner. The show was entertaining, and the smells from the cookpots on the stove and in the oven really whetted their appetites. At 7:45, the food was ready. The chef served all 20 guests from the counter, buffet-style, which was how it was done in his home country.

The *Beef and Guinness Stew* was fragrant and

hearty, with chunks of rough-cut potatoes, carrots, boneless beef chuck, onions, bacon, celery, spices and seasonings, and, of course, Guinness beer. Accompanying the stew was the traditional brown Irish soda bread, with Kerrygold butter and Dubliner cheese. When all of them had been served, the chef lifted a glass of dark Guinness, and the guests followed suits.

"*Sláinte!*" Chef Finbar Holmes said. "That's 'health' in Gaelic."

"*Sláinte!*" his guests echoed.

After dinner, Earl helped Tommie to her feet and put his arm around her waist. Thanking chef Finbar, they exited the restaurant. Tommie looked back and read the lighted marquis over the two side-by-side establishments and smiled.

Watson's Herbal Teas & Potions

NOTE: PLEASE HEED THE WARNINGS IN [BRACKETS!]
USED INCORRECTLY, HERBS CAN BE DEADLY AS POISONS!

TO MAKE TEA: Unless otherwise noted, measure equal amounts of each herb and combine in a large bowl. Mix thoroughly. Fill one tea strainer or infuser ball with 1-2 TBS of herb mixture and put in cup or mug. Pour 6-8 ounces of boiled water over the herbs and allow to steep for 5-10 minutes. Remove herbs. Add sweeteners, cream, or lemon as desired. *(Any herb may be omitted. For stronger tea, you may bruise or grind the herbs before adding. Be sure to store herbs in an airtight container away from heat and light. Tommie encourages the use of natural or organic sweeteners.)*

Natural or Organic Sweeteners

100% grade A dark maple syrup
Agave - blue, red, or gold
Raw honey
Vanilla
Stevia
Molasses
Monk fruit
Coconut sugar
Raw turbinado sugar
Cinnamon/all-spice/nutmeg

Laid-Back Landlord

Basil leaves

Lemon balm

Lavender flowers

[AVOID if pregnant or breastfeeding; omit if headache or constipation occur]

Cardamom (just a pinch!)

[IN MODERATION if pregnant or breastfeeding, or with gallstones]

Chamomile flowers

*[AVOID if pregnant or breastfeeding, if allergic to daisies or ragweed,
or with high blood pressure or cardiovascular disease;
can cause drowsiness, so avoid driving or operating machinery]*

Dreamer Creamer

Combine ingredients and refrigerate before use.

Fresh milk or cream, 8 oz

Nutmeg, ½ tsp, ground

Rose water, 1 TBS

[AVOID if pregnant or breastfeeding]

Honey-Honey

*Combine and let sit for 2-3 days. When ready to use,
pour into a cup and set in a pan of hot water.
Strain out blossoms before using in tea.*

Honeysuckle blossoms, fresh or dried

Raw clover honey

Blues Reme-Tea

Spearmint leaves

Lemon balm

Basil leaves

Oregano
[AVOID if pregnant or breastfeeding]
Nettle leaves
[CAUTION: fresh herb can sting skin; use dried herb for tea]
St. John's wort
[AVOID if pregnant or breastfeeding, or if taking antidepressants; can cause photosensitivity]

Fruity Friendship

Honeybush tea
Chopped dried apricots cherries, peaches
(can use any dried fruit of choice)
Cinnamon sticks, broken into small pieces

Romantic Red

Red Rooibos tea
Jasmine flowers
[AVOID if pregnant or breastfeeding]
Red rose buds
[AVOID if pregnant or breastfeeding; omit if headache occurs]
Mint leaves
(hand-tie around jasmine before steeping)

Zzzzz-Tea

Lemon balm
Hibiscus flowers
Spearmint leaves (2)
Rose petals (½)
[AVOID if pregnant or breastfeeding; omit if headache occurs]
Chamomile flowers
[AVOID if pregnant or breastfeeding, if allergic to daisies or ragweed,

or if high blood pressure or cardiovascular disease;
Can cause drowsiness, so avoid driving or operating machinery]

Teadle-Dee

Lemon balm
Peppermint leaves
Marshmallow leaves
Blackberry leaves
[AVOID with anticancer supplements/herbs]
Lavender flowers
[AVOID if pregnant or breastfeeding; omit if headache or constipation occur]

Teadle-Dum

Thyme (¼)
Lemon peel
Spearmint leaves
Red clover herb and blossoms
[AVOID if on blood thinners or heart medications;
AVOID 2 weeks before or after surgery.]

Queen of Hearts

Jasmine blossoms
[AVOID if pregnant or breastfeeding]
Red rose petals
[AVOID if pregnant or breastfeeding; omit if headache occurs]
Raspberry leaves
[AVOID if pregnant or breastfeeding, or with uterine fibroids,
hormone-related cancers, or endometriosis]
Green tea leaves
(hand-tie around jasmine before steeping)

Cheshire Cat Coffee

*(roast ingredients on a sheet pan in 350° oven
until dark brown; cool and grind before use)*

Chicory

Mocha mix

(Raw cocoa nibs, carob, and/or raw chocolate)

Dandelion root

[AVOID with gallstones or with seasonal allergies to dandelions]

Tommie's Valentine Treats

Besame Bagel Bites

INGREDIENTS:
Premade or refrigerated bagels
Milk, ½ cup
Sugar, ¼ cup
Butter, 1 TBS
Poppyseeds, 2 TBS

PREPARATION: Toast premade bagels or follow package directions on refrigerated bagels package. Cool on racks. DRIZZLING SYRUP: Simmer milk and poppyseeds on low heat. Whisk in sugar and butter until all ingredients melt and combined. Remove from heat. Drizzle over cooled bagels.

Salty Sweetheart Mix

INGREDIENTS:
Fig filled cookies, quartered
Dark chocolate pieces
Cranberries, dried
Pumpkin seeds
Pretzel bits
Butter mints

PREPARATION: Combine equal portions of all ingredients in a large zipper lock bag and shake gently to distribute sweet and salty elements. Portion into cups, bags, or small bowls to serve.

Double Sweet Kisses

INGREDIENTS:
Peanut butter, smooth or crunchy
Hershey's Kisses
Milk chocolate

PREPARATION: Lay chocolate kisses flat side down on baking sheet. Holding the tip, spread peanut butter all around the sides. Freeze on trays until hard. Heat milk chocolate in a double boiler or in a glass dish in the microwave, stirring frequently until melted. Transfer frozen candies to crisscrossed cooling racks over baking sheets. Spoon melted chocolate over kisses and put in refrigerator (or freezer) until ready to serve.

Culinary Creations by Holmes

Even though Finbar Holmes is from Ireland, all ingredients listed in his recipes are measured in standard United States customary units. Feel free to add, omit, or substitute ingredients in the proper ratios.

Irish Soda Bread

INGREDIENTS:
All-purpose wheat flour, 4 cups
Baking soda, I tsp
Salt, I tsp
Buttermilk, I ½ cups

PREPARATION: Preheat oven to 425°. Sift and whisk together flour, baking soda, and salt. Form a well in the center of the flour mixture and pour in buttermilk, Blend together using hands until the texture is crumbly but sticks together and pulls away from the bowl. Form into a ball and place on a greased cast iron skillet or in a Dutch oven. Make an "X" across the top of the dough with a sharp knife, just about an inch or so deep. Bake for 40 minutes until outside is browned. To serve, slice with a bread knife and top with an Irish butter (like *Kerrygold*) and sliced strong cheese (like *Kerrygold Dubliner, Blarney Castle, Aged Cheddar, Ballyshannon,* or *Skellig.*)

Fish & Chips with Mushy Peas & Malt Vinegar

INGREDIENTS: (4 SERVINGS)
Marrowfat dried peas, 1 cup
Baking soda, 1 ½ tsp
Salt, ½ tsp
White large flake fish (cod, scamp, pollock, haddock), 4 filets
All-purpose flour, 1 ½ cups
Salt, 1 tsp
Beer or ale, 14.9 oz. (Guinness, or use a non-alcoholic ale)
Peanut or other high temperature oil for frying
Potatoes, 4 large russet
Salt, to taste
Malt Vinegar

PREPARATION - PEAS: Combine dried peas and baking soda in a pot. Cover with water and bring to a boil. Remove from heat, cover pot, and soak peas for two or more hours. Rinse well and return to pot. Cover with water, add salt, and simmer covered for an hour until peas thicken and are mushy.

PREPARATION – FISH: Whisk together 1 cup flour, salt, and beer and set aside. Heat oil in a Dutch oven to 375° or until a bit of batter sizzles when dropped in. Pat fish dry, then toss in remaining ½ cup flour and shake off excess. Dip filet in the beer batter and let the excess drip off. Carefully lower fish into hot oil about halfway and hold for 15 seconds, then drop it in and cook until golden brown, about 7 or 8 minutes. Drain on a wire rack over a baking sheet. (can be kept warm by placing rack in a cold oven)

PREPARATION – CHIPS: Peel and rinse potatoes. Cut each

potato in half lengthwise, then cut each half in half. Continue halving the sections until you have 16 long rectangular wedges. Cover in water and bring to a boil, then reduce heat and simmer 3-4 minutes. Drain and dry with paper towels, then let them sit for 5-10 minutes in a colander. Lower a few at a time into the hot oil (yes, you can use the same oil) and fry until they are a golden brown. Drain on a wire rack and sprinkle liberally with salt. Serve with a good malt vinegar (like Heinz).

Rissole

INGREDIENTS:
(usually made from leftovers!)
Potatoes, boiled or fried
Fish, minced (or other minced meat)
Onion, diced
Salt and pepper, to taste
Breadcrumbs or flour
Peanut or other high temperature oil for frying

PREPARATION: Heat oil in a Dutch oven to 375° or until a bit of flour sizzles when dropped in. Combine all ingredients except breadcrumbs/flour in a bowl and mash together. Scoop up with hands and fashion into golf ball sized portions. Either leave round or flatten slightly. Roll in breadcrumbs/flour. Drop into hot oil and fry until golden brown.

Colcannon

INGREDIENTS:
Red or Yukon gold potatoes, 1-¼ lbs
Cabbage, 1 small head, chopped

Green onions, ½ cup, chopped
Irish butter, 6 TBS
Salt and pepper, to taste

Preparation: Rinse and quarter potatoes (with or without skins). Cover potatoes, cabbage, and onions with water by at least an inch in a Dutch oven and bring to a boil. Add a pinch of salt and simmer covered until fork tender, about 20 minutes. Drain and place in a large bowl. Mash potatoes and vegetables with butter until the mixture is chunky. Season with salt and pepper to serve. (Note: leftover Colcannon can be used to make Rissole!)

Late-for-a-Date Tea Biscuits

INGREDIENTS:
Butter, 1 cup softened
Sugar, 2 cups
Eggs, 3 large
Vanilla Extract, 1 tsp
All-purpose flour, 3 ½ cups
(can use whole wheat or almond flour, if desired)
Baking soda, 1 tsp
Salt, ½ tsp
Dates, ¼ cup chopped

PREPARATION: Heat oven to 350°. Cream butter on medium speed with electric mixer. Add sugar gradually. Add eggs, one at a time. Add vanilla. Be sure all are blended well. In a bowl, combine flour, baking soda, and salt. Gradually add to butter mixture until well blended. Divide dough and wrap each half in plastic wrap. Chill 1 hour. Roll each half to ¼-inch thickness on floured surface. Cut cookies with a 2 ½-inch round cutter. Bake for 10-12 minutes until edges begin to brown. Rest on baking sheets for 5 minutes. While still warm, use a toothpick to press 12 notches around the sides like a clockface. Place date pieces onto the 12, 3, 6, and 9 notches. Cool on wire racks.

Mad Hatter Muffins

INGREDIENTS:
All-purpose flour, 1 ¼ cups
(can use whole wheat or almond flour, if desired)
olled oats, ¼ cup
Light brown sugar, 1 cup
Baking soda, ½ tsp
Orange, 1 medium, juiced and zested
Oil, 1 TBS sunflower or other light vegetable oil
Yogurt, 1 cup plain
Egg, 1 large
Marmalade, ¼ cup chunky
(or other chunky fruit preserve)

PREPARATION: Heat oven to 400°. Prepare large, regular, or small sized muffin tin by lightly greasing, coating with nonstick spray, or with paper baking cups. Combine flour, oats, sugar, baking powder, and baking soda in a bowl. In another bowl, whisk orange juice and zest, oil, yogurt, and egg. Fold into dry mixture until combined. Spoon 1 TBS (depending on size of muffin tin compartments) into each muffin compartment. Top with 1 tsp. orange marmalade, then cover with remaining muffin mixture. Bake for 15-20 minutes until golden brown on top.

March Hare Madeleines

INGREDIENTS:
Butter, ½ cup softened plus extra melted
Coconut, 2 ½ cups shredded
Sugar, ¾ cup
All-purpose flour, 1 ¼ cup
(can use whole wheat or almond flour, if desired)
g, 1 large
Yogurt, 1 cup vanilla
Dried fruit, ¾ cup chopped

Preparation: Heat oven to 325°. Grease madeleine molds with butter. Use a food processor or hand chop coconut until fine. Whisk together with butter, flour, egg, and yogurt until smooth. Fold in fruit. Fill molds ¾ full and bake on a baking sheet for 35-45 minutes or until a toothpick comes out clean when inserted. Cool for 10 minutes. Brush with melted butter and dust with a bit of the sugar/coconut mixture. Madeleines can also be brushed with a thin coating of jam before serving.

Dormouse Delights

INGREDIENTS – CRUST:
All-purpose flour, 1 ½ cups
(can use whole wheat or almond flour, if desired)
Butter, ¾ cup, cold diced
Powdered sugar, ¼ cup
Lemon, 1 zested
INGREDIENTS – FILLING:

Eggs, 4 large
Powdered sugar, 1 cup
Lemons, ½ cup juice
All-purpose flour, 2 TBS
Lemon, sliced into small flat quarter rounds

PREPARATION: Heat oven to 350°. Line 8x8 baking pan with parchment paper. Combine crust ingredients and cut in butter until the mixture resembled fine crumbles. Sprinkle evenly into pan and press to form an even crust. Bake for 20 minutes or until light golden brown. Whisk filling ingredients together until combined. As soon as crust is done, remove from oven and pour lemon filling on top of hot crust. Bake for 18-20 minutes more, or until the filling has set. Cool on a rack until room temperature, then chill for 2 hours. To serve, cut into small triangles and top with a quarter round lemon slice.

Beef and Guinness Stew

INGREDIENTS:
Bacon, 4 slices chopped
Boneless beef chuck, 2 ½ lbs cut into 2-inch cubes
Salt and pepper, to taste
Onions, 2 coarsely chopped
Carrots, 3 cut into 2-inch pieces
Celery, 2 stalks cut into 2-inch pieces
Potatoes, 4 Russet, cut into 2-inch cubes
Garlic, 4 cloves minced
Tomato paste, ¼ cup
Guinness Beer, 14.9 ounces
Thyme, 4 sprigs fresh

Sugar, I tsp

Chicken or beef stock, 2 ½ cups or enough to cover by I inch

Preparation: In a Dutch oven, cook bacon until browned. Remove and set aside in a bowl, leaving fat. Season beef with salt and pepper. Turn heat to high and brown in bacon fat about 5 minutes. Remove to bowl. Turn down heat and sauté onions and garlic in the remainder of the fat about I minute. Add beef and bacon, along with remainder of ingredients, except potatoes. Bring to a boil, stirring constantly to incorporate browned bits from the bottom of the pot, then reduce to a simmer. Cover and simmer for I ½ hours, stirring occasionally. Remove cover and add potatoes. Raise heat to medium and bring to a low boil for 20-30 minutes, until potatoes are fork tender. Remove from heat and let sit covered for 15 minutes. Serve in a bowl with brown bread and butter.

HOLMES & WATSON

INVESTIGATIVE CASE FILES

TAINTED TEACUP

Solved March 1, 2019

Finbar Holmes, Thomasina Watson

CRIME: DEATH IN WATSON'S TEA SHOP

2ND DEATH IN BREWSTER'S COFFEE SHOP!!

VICTIM: MS. CORAL BEADWELL ~~PROZAK, CELEXA,~~

WEAPON: POISON (CYANIDE) ~~HALDOL, TAGAMET~~

METHOD: ADMINISTERED IN TEACUP (in 2ND V's coffee mug)

DATE/TIME: MONDAY, FEB. 11, 2019 12:28 P.M.

Thursday, Feb. 14, 2019 7:00 a.m. (Beverly Cantrell)

DISCOVERED: FLOOR OF WATSON'S REME-TEAS.

DISCOVERED BY: THOMASINA WATSON (Henry, Holmes)

→ Beverly died in Brewster's Coffee Shoppe - witnesses **

PRESENT: ** THOMASINA WATSON (served 1st V)

　　　　　　** CHARLES WILLIAMS

　　　　DON LAREBY　　　** Finbar Holmes (2nd)

　　　　SUSAN CLAY　　　(siblings)

　　　　ELAINE FRANK

(2nd victim) ** BEVERLY CANTRELL (before and after)

(w/2ND)　** HENRY ERVING (after)

　　　　** LINDA BEADWELL (before)

(served 2nd V)　'* SARAH BETH BREWSTER (next door)

DESCRIPTION OF VICTIM: CORAL BEADWELL

Age 58, 1.65 meters/5'5", 180 lbs, grey hair worn in low

ponytail, blue eyes, square black framed glasses, pale

blue UPS shirt, khaki slacks, no makeup, face flushed

just prior to death

SUSPECT DESCRIPTIONS

1. CHARLES WILLIAMS

    Age 49, heavyset, 6' tall +/-, 190 lbs, dark black hair,
    dark brown eyes, thin mustache, round wire-rimmed glasses

2. DON LAREBY

    (41)
    Age early 40s, slender, <6' tall, brown hair, ~~tight~~ amber brown eyes,

    wears suits, quiet man, works at First Floribunda Bank

    Brother of Susan Clay and Elaine Frank

3. SUSAN CLAY

    (45, 200 lbs)   amber brown
    Age mid 40s, heavy, 5'7", brown hair, ~~tight~~ eyes, works

    at First Bank of Floribunda (twin sister of Elaine Frank)

4. ELAINE FRANK

    (45, 200 lbs)   amber brown
    Age mid 40s, heavy, 5'7", brown hair, ~~tight~~ eyes, works

    at First Bank of Floribunda (twin sister of Susan Clay)

5. HENRY ~~IRVING~~ ERVING

    (61, 185, 6'1")
    Age early 60s, 6'1"-6'2", medium build, paunch belly,
    Lt. blue
    light hair, ~~pale~~ eyes, ruddy complexion, wide hips, hairy

    knuckles, works UPS Store (w/Coral Beadwell)

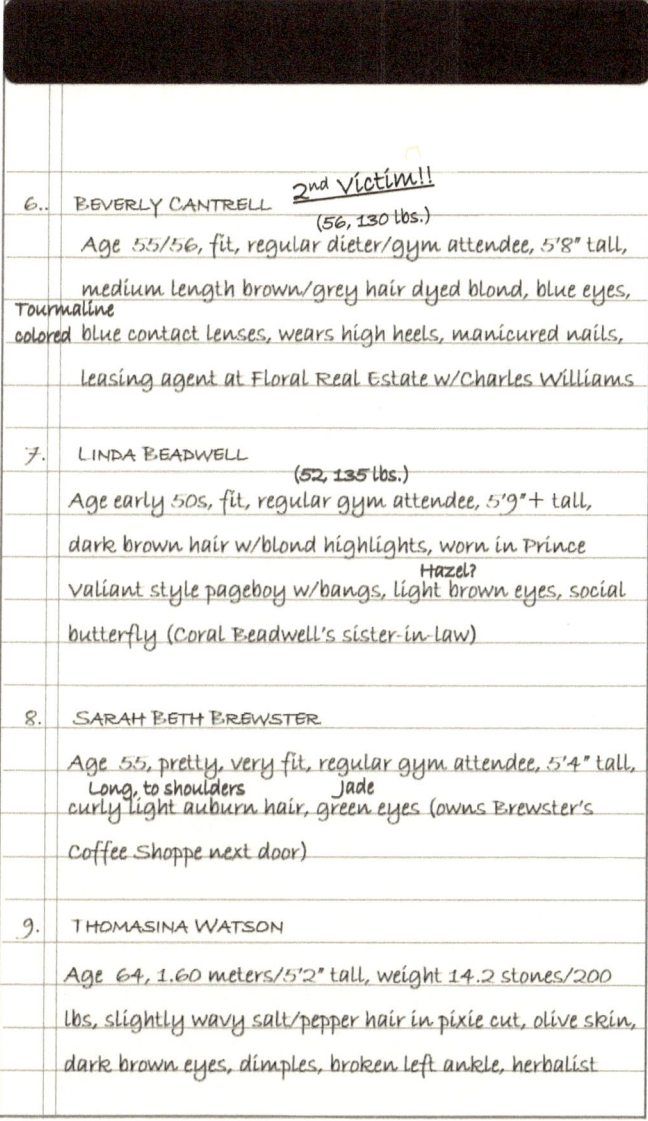

6.. BEVERLY CANTRELL   2nd Victim!!
       (56, 130 lbs.)
       Age 55/56, fit, regular dieter/gym attendee, 5'8" tall,

       medium length brown/grey hair dyed blond, blue eyes,
Tourmaline
colored blue contact lenses, wears high heels, manicured nails,

       leasing agent at Floral Real Estate w/Charles Williams

7. LINDA BEADWELL
       (52, 135 lbs.)
    Age early 50s, fit, regular gym attendee, 5'9"+ tall,

    dark brown hair w/blond highlights, worn in Prince
                          Hazel?
    Valiant style pageboy w/bangs, light brown eyes, social

    butterfly (Coral Beadwell's sister-in-law)

8. SARAH BETH BREWSTER

    Age 55, pretty, very fit, regular gym attendee, 5'4" tall,
    Long, to shoulders   jade
    curly light auburn hair, green eyes (owns Brewster's

    Coffee Shoppe next door)

9. THOMASINA WATSON

    Age 64, 1.60 meters/5'2" tall, weight 14.2 stones/200

    lbs, slightly wavy salt/pepper hair in pixie cut, olive skin,

    dark brown eyes, dimples, broken left ankle, herbalist

OUTSIDE RESOURCES

1. SANDERSON HARPER

   County Coroner, Tommie Watson's cousin, owns the

   shops leased by Tommie & Sarah Beth, goes to First

   Presbyterian Church w/Charles Williams

   Description: 63, 5'10", 210 lbs., dark salt/pepper hair, dk. Brown
   eyes, black frame glasses, middle-age spread

2. EARL PETRY

   Officer, Floribunda Police Department, lived In

   Floribunda his whole life, knows most everyone, he and

   Tommie have a mutual attraction for one another

   Description: 58, 6'2", 200 lbs, silver crew cut, blue/grey eyes, white
   beard, Muscular, olive complexion (tanned)

3. DON LAREBY, SUSAN CLAY, ELAINE FRANK

   Work at First Floribunda Bank, town gossips, know all

   the dirt on everybody, like Finbar and Tommie, regular

   customers of Watson's

SUSPECT INTERVIEWS

SUSPECT 1: SARAH BETH BREWSTER

INTERVIEWED AT: BREWSTER'S COFFEE SHOPPE

MOTIVE:

1. Revenge - CORAL cost her business w/Trinity Church

2. Greed - Discredit TOMMIE, take over her lease to expand coffee shop

3. MISDIRECTION - Bev's death

ALIBI: Closed early for groceries & to avoid Charles Williams.

LIES:

1. Must verify reasons for tardiness & early closure

TRUTHS:

1. Closed early

2. sent Linda Beadwell out back

IMPLICATES: Charles Williams, Linda Beadwell

GOSSIP & HEARSAY:

1. Charles & Linda affair
2. Husband bipolar - takes Haldol
3. Son depressed - takes Celexa
4. OCD - takes PROZAK

QUESTIONS:

1. details of argument?
2. why late opening?

OBSERVATIONS:

1. Has a key & access to shop
2. Cannot take over Tommie's lease, it is family property

SUSPECT INTERVIEWS

SUSPECT 2: HENRY ERVING

INTERVIEWED AT: UPS STORE

MOTIVE:

1. Loss of income - passed over for promotion, Coral's fault
2. Humiliation/Revenge - Coral threw his gift away in front of coworkers.
3. Jealousy - unrequited love

ALIBI: Eating lunch in gazebo w/Beverly Cantrell 12:05-12:28

LIES:

1. Beverly was his girlfriend?
2. Had a date w/Beverly for lunch
3. Was not stalking Coral

TRUTHS:

1. Watched Coral & Charles go into shop together
2. Brought Bev to coffee shop, bought her coffee
3. Knew about drugs from Mexico (Coral); gave bag to Bev to lock in desk drawer

IMPLICATES: Charles Williams & himself

GOSSIP & HEARSAY:

1. Hopelessly smitten w/Coral

QUESTIONS:

1. Relationship with Coral Beadwell? (love/hate)
2. Relationship with Beverly Cantrell? (rebound)

OBSERVATIONS:

1. No access to teacups
2. Touched poisoned napkins & cup; got sick
3. Seemed genuinely upset about Beverly's death

SUSPECT INTERVIEWS

SECOND VICTIM!

SUSPECT 3: BEVERLY CANTRELL

INTERVIEWED AT: FLORAL REAL ESTATE

MOTIVE:

1. Jealousy - wanted CORAL out of the way so she could have a relationship with Henry

2. Greed - big commission if CORAL dead & house sells

3. Greed - leasing fees if TOMMIE has to rent new house

ALIBI: Eating lunch in gazebo w/Henry Erving 12:05-12:28

LIES:

1. No date w/Henry; he was not her boyfriend

TRUTHS:

1. In the gazebo w/Henry when Coral died

2. Saw Charles & Coral walk to shop & go in together

IMPLICATES: Charles Williams

GOSSIP & HEARSAY:

1. Did NOT have relationship w/Henry
2. Split commission w/Charles on Beadwell House sale when Coral bought it, stands to split another if Tom & Linda buy it.

QUESTIONS:

1. How long relationship w/Henry? (a day or two after Coral died)

OBSERVATIONS:

1. Touched the teacups
2. Got water & tea from cooler
3. Knew Coral had a favorite cup
4. Freely drank the coffee bought by Henry
5. Died – same way as Coral but in Brewster's

SUSPECT INTERVIEWS

SUSPECT 4: CHARLES WILLIAMS

INTERVIEWED AT: FLORAL REAL ESTATE

MOTIVE:

1. Revenge - Coral damaged his packages, he hated her
2. Greed - discredit Tommie to gain control of her shop

ALIBI: Sitting away from Coral when she died

Nowhere near Beverly when she died

LIES:

1. Did not have relationship w/ MRS. Beadwell

TRUTHS:

1. Walked over with Coral & they entered together
2. Saw Henry in gazebo at 12:00
3. Not with Coral

IMPLICATES: Tommie Watson

GOSSIP & HEARSAY:

1. Split commission w/Beverly on Beadwell House sale when Coral bought it, stands to split another if Tom & Linda buy it.
2. Receiving illegal drugs from Mexico, selling them

QUESTIONS:

1. Relationship with Coral Beadwell? (hated her)
2. Why he came to the shop with her? (she initiated it)
3. Why did he threaten her? (blackmailing him about drugs)

OBSERVATIONS:

1. grabbed Coral's teacup
2. Threatened Coral in the shop
3. Argued w/Coral and had a damaged package
4. Denied having a relationship with MRS. Beadwell (not Coral) - a Freudian ship of the tongue?

SUSPECT INTERVIEWS

SUSPECT 5: LINDA BEADWELL

INTERVIEWED AT: ST. MARY'S CATHOLIC CHURCH (BINGO)

MOTIVE:

1. Conspiracy - help Charles discredit Tommie
2. Greed - wanted Beadwell House for herself
3. Greed - could recoup part of sale from Charles' commission

ALIBI: Left Brewster's before Tommie opened shop (lie)

LIES:

1. Was nowhere near Tommie's shop
2. Had to use the bathroom (home 3 blocks away)

TRUTHS:

1. Watched Coral & Charles walking across street
2. Admitted she would be living in the main house
3. Didn't want Charles to see her spying on him

IMPLICATES: Tommie Watson

GOSSIP & HEARSAY:

1. Affair w/Charles Williams
2. Tom (Coral's brother) can buy Beadwell House if Coral is dead
3. Husband is pharmacist - access to drugs
4. Husband's daughter takes Prozac

QUESTIONS:

1. Why was she - coffee drinker - in Tommie's shop?
2. Affair w/Charles? (yes)
3. Did she go near the counter or cups? (yes)
4. "We're" glad you're closed down? Who is "we"? (she & Charles)

OBSERVATIONS:

1. Hiding in bathroom
2. Tommie couldn't see her from inside the display - could've touched Coral's cup. admitted she saw them.

☆ CONTRIBUTING FACTORS: Sarah Beth OCD;
husband abusive, bipolar; son depressed, suicidal.

SOLUTION

KILLER: SARAH BETH BREWSTER

MOTIVE:

FOR KILLING CORAL - No motive for killing Coral; she was

just the one who got the cup she poisoned

FOR IMPLICATING TOMMIE - GREED - She wanted to

discredit her so she'd lose the shop, then Sarah Beth could

take over the lease and have a larger business

* She did not intend to kill the first victim

NOTE: She did not know the shop was Harper
family property and could not be sold!

MOTIVE:

FOR KILLING BEVERLY - No motive for killing Beverly; she

was just the one who got the mug when it got busy.

* Charles was the intended victim   She planned to kill Charles!

FOR IMPLICATING HERSELF - MISDIRECTION - She

wanted to appear she was being targeted to throw

attention away from herself

MOTIVE:

FOR ATTACKING TOMMIE - PANIC - came into shop to

poison another cup; didn't want Tommie to see her so she

knocked her out with the pestle   Almost Killed Tommie!

MOTIVE:

FOR TRYING TO POISON TOMMIE - GREED/COVERUP - get Tommie's shop; keep Tommie from discovering she was the killer

She planned to kill Tommie, at the reopening before she realized what an impact Tommie made in Barry's life.

METHOD:

1. Ground up her family's mental health medications and put them in the cup & the mug

MEANS:

1. Had a key to Watson's. Slipped in before 6 a.m. to dose a cup, didn't know it was Coral's cup; when she heard Linda knocking on her door, she panicked and put too much poison in.

2. Set aside a mug in her shop for Charles. When the rush came, she grabbed it by mistake for Beverly

3. Dosed Tommie's cup before the reopening.

TURNING POINT:

1. Tommie proved she was a true friend

2. Tommie was kind to Sarah Beth's son

DISPENSATION: imprisonment, mental health facility

Barry checked into rehab center. Kevin Watson befriending him. Now that mother/father out of his life, there may be hope for this young man once he gets the professional help he desperately needs!

About the Author

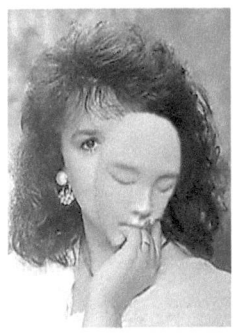

MICHELLE BUSBY is a Florida transplant who lived for a time in California where she was an actress, singer, and writer and a member of the American Federation of Television and Radio Artists (AFTRA). A life-long thespian and former teacher, she has performed on stage since her teens and has written plays, musicals, and novels for all ages under the pen names of Mickey MorningGlory, Mickey Middleton, and M.M. Busby. An avid puzzle solver, mystery buff, and self-proclaimed foodie, she combines her talents into one large pot where she stews up her Holmes and Watson Culinary Whodunits. She is a member of *Sisters in Crime (SinC)*, *Women's Fiction Writers Association (WFWA)*, *National Association of Independent Writers and Editors (NAIWE)*, *American Copy Editors Society (ACES)*, and *Society of Children's Book Writers and Illustrators (SCBWI)*. Michelle lives in Florida with her family.

Readers can visit Michelle at patentprintbooks.com.